GOOD
WIVES

. . . he played the " Sonata Pathetique " . . .

[see page 80

FOULSHAM'S BOY AND GIRL FICTION LIBRARY

GOOD WIVES

A SEQUEL TO LITTLE WOMEN

By

LOUISA M. ALCOTT

WITH FIVE COLOUR PLATES BY
HARRY FRICKER

LONDON:
W. FOULSHAM & CO., LTD.
NEW YORK   TORONTO   CAPE TOWN   SYDNEY

MADE IN GREAT BRITAIN
by C. TINLING & CO., LTD.,
LIVERPOOL, LONDON & PRESCOT
ABRIDGED EDITION
18E

CONTENTS

LIST OF COLOUR PLATES

GOOD WIVES

CHAPTER I

GOSSIP

In order that we may go to Meg's wedding with free minds, it will be well to begin with a little gossip about the Marchs.

The three years that have passed have brought but few changes to the quiet family. The war is over, and Mr. March safely at home, busy with his books and the small parish which found in him a minister by nature as by grace. These attributes attracted to him many admirable persons, as naturally as sweet herbs draw bees, and as naturally he gave them the honey into which fifty years of hard experience had distilled no bitter drop, and even worldlings confessed that his beliefs were beautiful and true, although "they wouldn't pay."

Mrs. March is as brisk and cheery, though rather greyer than when we saw her last, and just now so absorbed in Meg's affairs, that the hospitals and homes, still full of wounded "boys" and soldiers' widows, decidedly miss the motherly missionary's visits.

John Brooke did his duty manfully for a year, got wounded, was sent home, and not allowed to return. Resigned to his discharge, he devoted himself to getting well, preparing for business, and earning a home for Meg. With the good sense and sturdy independence that characterised him, he refused Mr. Laurence's more generous offers, and accepted the place of under book-keeper, feeling better satisfied to begin with an honestly-earned salary, than by running any risks with borrowed money.

Meg had spent the time in working as well as waiting, growing womanly in character, wise in housewifery arts, and prettier than ever; for love is a great beautifier. Ned Moffat had just married Sallie Gardner, and Meg couldn't help contrasting their fine house and splendid

outfit with her own, and secretly wishing she could have
the same.   But somehow envy and discontent soon vanished
when she thought of all the patient love and labour John
had put into the little home awaiting her ; and when they
sat together in the twilight, talking over their small plans,
she forgot Sallie's splendour, and felt herself the richest,
happiest girl in Christendom.

Jo never went back to Aunt March, for the old lady
took such a fancy to Amy that she bribed her with the
offer of drawing lessons from one of the best teachers
going ; and for the sake of this advantage, Amy would
have served a far harder mistress.   Jo, meantime, devoted
herself to literature and Beth, who remained delicate
long after the fever was a thing of the past. As long as
" The Spread Eagle " paid her a dollar a column for her
" rubbish " as she called it, Jo felt herself a woman of
means, and spun her little romances diligently.   But great
plans fermented in her ambitious mind, and the garret
held a slowly increasing pile of blotted manuscript, which
was one day to place the name of March upon the roll of
fame.

Laurie, having dutifully gone to college to please his
grandfather, was now getting through it in the easiest
possible manner to please himself.   A universal favourite,
thanks to money, manners, much talent, and the kindest
heart that ever got its owner into scrapes by trying to
get other people out of them, he stood in great danger
of being spoilt, and probably would have been, like many
another promising boy, if he had not possessed a talisman
against evil in the memory of the kind old man who was
bound up in his success, the motherly friend who watched
over him as if he were her son, and last, but not least
by any means, the knowledge that four innocent girls
loved, admired, and believed in him with all their hearts.
The " men of my class " were heroes in the eyes of the girls,
who never wearied of the exploits of " our fellows," and
were frequently allowed to bask in the smiles of these
great creatures, when Laurie brought them home with him.

Amy especially enjoyed this high honour, and became
quite a belle among them ; for her ladyship early felt
and learned to use the gift of fascination with which she
was endowed.   Meg was too much absorbed in her private
and particular John to care for any other lords of creation,

and Beth too shy to do more than peep at them, and wonder how Amy dared to order them about so ; but Jo felt quite in her element, and found it very difficult to refrain from imitating the gentlemanly attitudes, phrases, and feats which seemed more natural to her than the decorums prescribed for young ladies. They all liked Jo immensely, but never fell in love with her, though very few escaped without paying the tribute of a sentimental sigh or two at Amy's shrine. And speaking of sentiment brings us very naturally to the " Dovecote."

That was the name of the little brown house which Mr. Brooke had prepared for Meg's first home. It was a tiny house, with a little garden behind, and a lawn about as big as a pocket handkerchief in front. Inside, it was altogether charming, and the happy bride saw no fault from garret to cellar. To be sure the hall was so narrow it was fortunate that they had no piano, for one never could have been got in whole. The dining-room was so small, that six people were a tight fit, and the kitchen stairs seemed built for the express purpose of precipitating both servants and china pell-mell into the coal-bin. But once get used to these slight blemishes, and nothing could be more complete, for good sense and good taste had presided over the furnishing, and the result was highly satisfactory. There were no marbled-topped tables, long mirrors, or lace curtains in the little parlour, but simple furniture, plenty of books, a fine picture or two, a stand of flowers in the bay-window, and, scattered all about, the pretty gifts which came from friendly hands. I doubt if any young matron ever began life with so rich a supply of dusters, holders, and piece-bags, for Beth made enough to last till the silver wedding came round, and invented three different kinds of dishcloths for the express service of the bridal china.

What happy times they had planning together ; what solemn shopping excursions, what funny mistakes they made, and what shouts of laughter arose over Laurie's ridiculous bargains ! His last whim had been to bring with him, on his weekly visits, some new, useful, and ingenious article for the young housekeeper.

Everything was done at last, even to Amy's arranging different coloured soaps to match the different coloured rooms, and Beth's setting the table for the first meal.

"Are you satisfied? Does it seem like home, and do you feel as if you should be happy here?" asked Mrs. March, as she and her daughter went through the new kingdom, arm-in-arm—for just then they seemed to cling together more tenderly than ever.

"Yes, mother, perfectly satisfied, thanks to you all, and *so* happy that I can't talk about it," answered Meg, with a look that was better than words.

'If she only had a servant or two it would be all right," said Amy, coming out of the parlour, where she had been trying to decide whether the bronze Mercury looked best on the whatnot or the mantelpiece.

"Mother and I have talked that over, and I have made up my mind to try her way first. There will be so little to do, that, with Lotty to run my errands and help me here and there, I shall only have enough work to keep me from getting lazy or homesick," answered Meg, tranquilly.

"If Meg had four the house wouldn't hold them, and master and missis would have to camp in the garden," broke in Jo, who, enveloped in a big blue pinafore, was giving a last polish to the door handles.

"Sallie isn't a poor man's wife, and many maids are in keeping. Meg and John begin humbly, but I have a feeling that there will be quite as much happiness in the little house as in the big one. When I was first married I used to long for my new clothes to wear out, or get torn, so that I might have the pleasure of mending them; for I got heartily sick of doing fancy work and tending my pocket handkerchief. You begin the other end, Meg, dear, but the lessons you learn now will be of use to you by-and-by, when John is a richer man, for the mistress of a house, however splendid, should know how work *ought* to be done, if she wishes to be well and honestly served."

"Yes, mother, I'm sure of that," said Meg, listening respectfully to the little lecture; for the best of women will hold forth upon the all-absorbing subject of house-keeping. "Do you know I like this room best of all in my baby-house," added Meg, a minute after, as they went upstairs, and she looked into her well-stored linen closet.

Beth was there, laying the snowy piles smoothly on the shelves, and exulting over the goodly array. All three laughed as Meg spoke; for that linen closet was a joke

You see, having said that if Meg married "that Brooke" she shouldn't have a cent of her money, Aunt March was rather in a quandary, when time had appeased her wrath, and made her repent her vow. She never broke her word, and was much exercised in her mind how to get round it, and at last devised a plan whereby she could satisfy herself. Mrs. Carrol, Florence's mamma, was ordered to buy, have made and marked a generous supply of house and table linen, and send it as *her* present. All of which was faithfully done, but the secret leaked out, and was greatly enjoyed by the family ; for Aunt March tried to look utterly unconscious, and insisted that she could give nothing but the old-fashioned pearls, long promised to the first bride.

"That's a housewifely taste, which I am glad to see," said Mrs. March, patting the damask table-cloths with a truly feminine appreciation of their fineness.

"Toodles is coming," cried Jo from below, and they all went down to meet Laurie, whose weekly visit was an important event in their quiet lives.

A tall, broad-shouldered young fellow came tramping down the road at a great pace, walked over the low fence, without stopping to open the gate, straight up to Mrs. March, with both hands out, and a hearty—

"Here I am, mother ! "

As Laurie spoke, he delivered a brown paper parcel to Meg, pulled Beth's hair ribbon, stared at Jo's big pinafore, and fell into an attitude of mock rapture before Amy, then shook hands all round, and everyone began to talk.

"Where is John ? " asked Meg anxiously.

"Stopped to get the license for to-morrow, ma'am."

"Which side won the last match, Teddy ? " inquired Jo, who persisted in feeling an interest in manly sports despite her nineteen years.

"Ours, of course. Wish you'd been there to see."

"How is the lovely Miss Randal ? " asked Amy, with a significant smile.

"More cruel than ever ; don't you see how I'm pining away ? " and Laurie gave his broad chest a sounding slap, and heaved a melodramatic sigh.

"What's the last joke ? Undo the bundle and see, Meg," said Beth, eyeing the knobby parcel with curiosity.

" It's a useful thing to have in the house in case of fire or thieves," observed Laurie, as a small watchman's rattle appeared amid the laughter of the girls.

" Any time when John is away, and you get frightened, Mrs. Meg, just swing that out of the front window, and it will rouse the neighbourhood in a jiffy. Nice thing, isn't it ? " and Laurie gave them a sample of its powers that made them cover up their ears.

" There's gratitude for you ! Come Jo, don't desert a fellow. I'm in such a state of exhaustion I can't get home without help," said Laurie.

" Now, Teddy, I want to talk seriously to you about to-morrow," began Jo, as they strolled away together. " You *must* promise to behave well, and not cut up any pranks, and spoil our plans."

" Not a prank. I say Jo, how is grandpa this week ; pretty amiable ? "

" Very ; why, have you got into a scrape, and want to know how he'll take it ? " asked Jo, rather sharply.

" Now Jo, don't be suspicious ; I only want some money," said Laurie.

" You spend a great deal, Teddy."

" Bless you, *I* don't spend it ; it spends itself, somehow, and is gone before I know it."

" You are so generous and kind-hearted, that you let people borrow, and can't say ' No ' to any one. We heard about Henshaw, and all you did for him. If you always spent money in that way, no one would blame you," said Jo, warmly.

" Oh, he made a mountain out of a mole-hill. Don't lecture any more, there's a good soul ; I have enough all through the week, and like to enjoy myself when I come home. By the way, Jo, I think that little Parker is really getting desperate about Amy. He'd better nip his little passion in the bud, hadn't he ? " added Laurie, in a confidential, elder-brotherly tone, after a minute's silence.

" Of course he had ; we don't want any more marrying in this family for years to come. Mercy on us, what *are* the children thinking of ! " and Jo looked as much scandalised as if Amy and little Parker were not yet in their teens.

" It's a fast age, and I don't know what we are coming to, ma'am. You are a mere infant, but you'll go next, Jo, and we'll be left lamenting," said Laurie, shaking his head over the degeneracy of the times.

" Me! don't be alarmed; I'm too busy to be worried with nonsense, and I think it's dreadful to break up families; Meg's wedding has turned all our heads, and we talk of nothing but lovers and such absurdities."

Whatever his feelings might have been, Laurie found a vent for them in a long, low whistle, and the fearful prediction, as they parted at the gate—" Mark my words, Jo, you'll go next."

CHAPTER II

THE FIRST WEDDING

THE June roses over the porch, rejoicing in cloudless sunshine, climbed up to nod and smile at the sisters, as they dressed the bride. Meg looked very like a rose herself; for all that was best and sweetest in heart and soul seemed to bloom into her face that day, making it fair and tender, with a charm more beautiful than beauty. She had made her wedding gown herself, sewing into it the tender hopes and innocent romances of a girlish heart. Her sisters braided up her pretty hair, and the only ornaments she wore were the lilies of the valley, which " her John " liked best of all the flowers that grew.

" You *do* look just like our own dear Meg, only so very sweet and lovely that I should hug you if it wouldn't crumple your dress," cried Amy, surveying her with delight when all was done.

" Then I am satisfied. But please hug and kiss me, everyone, and don't mind my dress; I want a great many crumples of this sort put into it to-day"; and Meg opened her arms to her sisters, who clung about her with April faces, for a minute, feeling that the new love had not changed the old.

" Now I'm going to tie John's cravat for him, and then to stay a few minutes with father, quietly in the study"; and Meg ran down to perform these little ceremonies, and then follow her mother wherever she went, conscious that in spite of the smiles on the motherly face, there was a secret sorrow hidden in the motherly heart at the flight of the first bird from the nest.

There were to be no ceremonious performances ; everything was to be as natural and homelike as possible ; so when Aunt March arrived, she was scandalised to see the bride come running to welcome and lead her in, to find the bridegroom fastening up a garland that had fallen down, and to catch a glimpse of the paternal minister marching upstairs with a grave countenance, and a wine bottle under each arm.

" Upon my word, here's a state of things ! " cried the old lady, taking the seat of honour prepared for her, and settling the folds of her lavender *moiré* with a great rustle. " You oughtn't to be seen till the last minute, child."

" I'm not a show, aunty, and no one is coming to stare at me, to criticise my dress, or count the cost of my luncheon. I'm too happy to care what anyone says or thinks, and I'm going to have my little wedding just as I like it. John, dear, here's your hammer," and away went Meg to help " that man " in his highly improper employment.

Mr. Brooke didn't even say " Thank you," but as he stooped for the unromantic tool, he kissed his little bride behind the folding-door, with a look that made Aunt March whisk out her pocket-handkerchief, with a sudden dew in her sharp old eyes.

There was no bridal procession, but a sudden silence fell upon the room as Mr. March and the young pair took their places under the green arch. Mother and sisters gathered close, as if loth to give Meg up ; the fatherly voice broke more than once, which only seemed to make the service more beautiful and solemn ; the bridegroom's hand trembled visibly, and no one heard his replies ; but Meg looked straight up in her husband's eyes, and said, " I will ! " with such tender trust in her own face and voice, that her mother's heart rejoiced, and Aunt March sniffed audibly.

Jo did *not* cry, though she was very near it once, and was only saved from a demonstration by the consciousness that Laurie was staring fixedly at her, with a comical mixture of merriment and emotion in his wicked black eyes. Beth kept her face hidden on her mother's shoulder, but Amy stood like a graceful statue, with a most becoming ray of sunshine touching her white forehead and the flower in her hair.

It wasn't at all the thing, I'm afraid, but the minute she was fairly married, Meg cried, " The first kiss for Marmee ! " and turning, gave it with her heart on her lips. During the next fifteen minutes she looked more like a rose than ever, for everyone availed themselves of their privileges to the fullest extent, from Mr. Laurence to old Hannah, who fell upon her in the hall, crying, " Bless you, deary, a hundred times ! "

Everybody cleared up after that, and said something brilliant, or tried to, which did just as well, for laughter is ready when hearts are light. There was no display of gifts, for they were already in the little house, nor was there an elaborate breakfast, but a plentiful lunch of cake and fruit, dressed with flowers. Mr. Laurence and Aunt March shrugged and smiled at one another when water, lemonade, and coffee were found to be the only sorts of nectar which the three Hebes carried round. No one said anything, however, till Laurie, who insisted on serving the bride, appeared before her with a loaded salver in his hand, and a puzzled expression on his face.

" Has Jo smashed all the bottles by accident ? " he whispered, " or am I merely labouring under a delusion that I saw some lying about loose this morning ? "

" No ; your grandfather kindly offered us his best, and Aunt March actually sent some, but father put away a little for Beth, and despatched the rest to the Soldiers' Home. You know he thinks that wine should only be used in illness, and mother says that neither she nor her daughters will ever offer it to any young man under her roof."

Meg spoke seriously, and expected to see Laurie frown or laugh ; but he did neither—for after a quick look at her, he said, in his impetuous way, " I like that ; for I've seen enough harm done to wish other women would think as you do ! "

After lunch, people strolled about, by twos and threes, through house and garden, enjoying the sunshine without and within. Meg and John happened to be standing together in the middle of the grass-plot, when Laurie was seized with an inspiration which put the finishing touch to this unfashionable wedding.

" All the married people take hands and dance round the new-made husband and wife, as the Germans do, while we bachelors and spinsters prance in couples outside ! " cried Laurie, galloping down the path with Amy, with such infectious spirit and skill that everyone else followed their example without a murmur. Mr. and Mrs. March, Aunt and Uncle Carrol, began it ; others rapidly joined in ; even Sallie Moffat, after a moment's hesitation, threw her train over her arm, and whisked Ned into the ring. But the crowning joke was Mr. Laurence and Aunt March for when the stately old gentleman *chasséed* solemnly up to the old lady, she just tucked her cane under her arm, and hopped briskly away to join hands with the rest, and dance about the bridal pair, while the young folks pervaded the garden, like butterflies on a midsummer day.

Want of breath brought the impromptu ball to a close, and then people began to go.

" I wish you well, my dear ; I heartily wish you well ; but I think you'll be sorry for it," said Aunt March to Meg, adding to the bridegroom, as he led her to the carriage, " You've got a treasure, young man—see that you deserve it."

" That is the prettiest wedding I've been to for an age, Ned, and I don't see why, for there wasn't a bit of style about it," observed Mrs. Moffat to her husband, as they drove away.

" Laurie, my lad, if you ever want to indulge in this sort of thing, get one of those little girls to help you, and I shall be perfectly satisfied," said Mr. Laurence, settling himself in his easy-chair to rest, after the excitement of the morning.

" I'll do my best to gratify you, sir," was Laurie's unusually dutiful reply, as he carefully unpinned the posy Jo had put in his button-hole.

The little house was not far away, and the only bridal journey Meg had was the quiet walk with John, from the old home to the new. When she came down, looking like a pretty Quakeress, in her dove-coloured suit and straw bonnet tied with white, they all gathered about her to say " good-bye," tenderly.

" Don't feel that I am separated from you, or that I love you any the less for loving John so much," she said, clinging to her mother, with full eyes, for a moment.

" Thank you all for my happy wedding-day. Good-bye
good-bye ! "

They stood watching her with faces full of love, and
hope, and tender pride, as she walked away, leaning on
her husband's arm, with her hands full of flowers, and the
June sunshine brightening her happy face—and so Meg's
married life began.

CHAPTER III

ARTISTIC ATTEMPTS

IT takes people a long time to learn the difference between
talent and genius, especially ambitious young men and
women. Amy was learning this distinction through much
tribulation ; for, mistaking enthusiasm for inspiration,
she attempted every branch of art with youthful audacity.
For a long time there was a lull in the " mud pie " business,
and she devoted herself to the finest pen-and-ink drawing,
in which she showed such taste and skill, that her graceful
handiwork proved both pleasant and profitable. But
overstrained eyes soon caused pen and ink to be laid aside
for a bold attempt at poker-sketching. While this attack
lasted, the family lived in constant fear of a conflagration,
and Hannah never went to bed without a pail of water
and the dinner-bell at her door, in case of fire.

From fire to oil was a natural transition for burnt
fingers, and Amy fell to painting with undiminished
ardour. An artist friend fitted her out with his cast-off
palettes, brushes, and colours, and she daubed away,
producing pastoral and marine views, such as were never
seen on land or sea.

Charcoal portraits came next ; and the entire family
hung in a row, looking as wild and crocky as if just evoked
from a coal-bin. Softened into crayon sketches, they did
better ; for the likenesses were good, and Beth's hair,
Jo's nose, Meg's mouth, and Laurie's eyes were pronounced
" wonderfully fine." A return to clay and plaster followed,
and ghostly casts of her acquaintances haunted corners
of the house, or tumbled off closet shelves on to people's
heads.

B

If "genius is eternal patience," as Michael Angelo affirms, Amy certainly had some claim to the divine attribute, for she persevered in spite of all obstacles, failures, and discouragements, firmly believing that in time she should do something worthy to be called " high art."

She was learning, doing, and enjoying other things, meanwhile, for she had resolved to be an attractive and accomplished woman, even if she never became a great artist. Here she succeeded better ; for she was one of those happily created beings who please without effort, make friends everywhere, and take life so gracefully and easily, that less fortunate souls are tempted to believe that such are born under a lucky star. Everybody liked her, for among her good gifts was tact. She had an instinctive sense of what was pleasing and proper, always said the right thing to the right person, did just what suited the time and place, and was so self-possessed that her sisters used to say, " If Amy went to court without any rehearsal beforehand, she'd know exactly what to do."

" I want to ask a favour of you, mamma," Amy said, coming in with an important air, one day.

" Well, little girl, what is it ? " replied her mother, in whose eyes the stately young lady still remained " the baby."

" Our drawing class breaks up next week, and before the girls separate for the summer, I want to ask them out here for a day. They are wild to see the river, sketch the broken bridge, and copy some of the things they admire in my book. They have been very kind to me in many ways, and I am grateful ; for they are all rich, and know I am poor, yet they never made any difference."

" Why should they ? " and Mrs. March put the question with what the girls called her " Maria Theresa air."

" You know as well as I that it *does* make a difference with nearly everyone, so don't ruffle up like a dear, motherly hen, when your chickens get pecked by smarter birds ; the ugly duckling turned out a swan, you know " ; and Amy smiled without bitterness, for she possessed a happy temper and hopeful spirit.

Mrs. March laughed, and smoothed down her maternal pride, as she asked—

" Well, my swan, what is your plan ? "

" I should like to ask the girls out to lunch next week,

to take them a drive to the places they want to see—a row on the river, perhaps—and make a little artistic fête for them."

" That looks feasible. What do you want for lunch ? Cake, sandwiches, fruit and coffee, will be all that is necessary, I suppose ? "

" Oh dear, no ! we must have cold tongue and chicken, French chocolate and ice-cream besides. Not more than six or eight will probably come, so I shall hire a beach-waggon and borrow Mr. Laurence's cherry-bounce." (Hannah's pronunciation of *char-a-banc*.)

" All this will be expensive, Amy."

" Not very ; I've calculated the cost, and I'll pay for it myself."

" Don't you think, dear, that as these girls are used to such things, and the best we could do would be nothing new, that some simpler plan would be pleasanter to them, as a change, if nothing more, and much better for us than buying or borrowing what we don't need, and attempting a style not in keeping with our circumstances ? "

" I know that I can carry it out perfectly well, if you and the girls will help a little ; and I don't see why I can't, if I'm willing to pay for it," said Amy, with the decision which opposition was apt to change into obstinacy.

Mrs. March knew that experience was an excellent teacher, and, when it was possible, she left her children to learn alone the lessons which she would gladly have made easier, if they had not objected to taking advice.

" Very well, Amy ; if your heart is set upon it, I'll say no more. Talk it over with the girls, and whichever way you decide, I'll do my best to help you."

" Thanks, mother ; you are always *so* kind," and away went Amy to lay her plan before her sisters.

Meg agreed at once, and promised her aid—gladly offering anything she possessed, from her little house itself to her very best salt-spoons. But Jo frowned upon the whole project, and would have nothing to do with it at first.

" Why in the world should you spend your money, and turn the house upside down for a parcel of girls who don't care a sixpence for you ? I thought you had too much pride and sense to truckle to any mortal woman just because she wears French boots and rides in a *coupé* " said Jo, who, being called from the tragical climax of her novel, was not in the best mood for social enterprises.

" I *don't* truckle, and I hate being patronised as much as you do ! " returned Amy, indignantly, for the two still jangled when such questions arose. " The girls do care for me, and I for them, and there's a great deal of kindness, and sense, and talent among them, in spite of what you call fashionable nonsense. You don't care to make people like you, to go into good society, and cultivate your manners and tastes. I do, and I mean to make the most of every chance that comes."

Much against her will, Jo at length consented to sacrifice a day to Mrs. Grundy, and help her sister through what she regarded as " a nonsensical business."

The invitations were sent, most all accepted, and the following Monday was set apart for the grand event. Hannah was out of humour because her week's work was deranged, and the cooking didn't turn out well ; the chicken was tough, the tongue too salt, and the chocolate wouldn't froth properly. Beth got cold, and took to bed ; Meg had an unusual number of callers to keep her at home, and Jo was in such a divided state of mind that her breakages and mistakes were uncommonly trying.

" If it hadn't been for mother I never should have got through," as Amy declared afterward, and gratefully remembered, when " the best joke of the season " was entirely forgotten by everybody else.

If it was not fair on Monday, the young ladies were to come on Tuesday, an arrangement which aggravated Jo and Hannah to the last degree. On Monday morning the weather was in that undecided state which is more exasperating than a steady pour. It drizzled a little, shone a little, blew a little, and didn't make up its mind till it was too late for anyone else to make up theirs. Amy was up at dawn, hustling people out of their beds and through their breakfasts, that the house might be got in order.

The lunch looked charmingly ; and, as she surveyed it, she sincerely hoped it would taste good, and that the borrowed glass, china, and silver would get safely home again.

Then came two hours of suspense, during which she

vibrated from parlour to porch, while public opinion varied like the weathercock. A smart shower, at eleven, had evidently quenched the enthusiasm of the young ladies who were to arrive at twelve, for nobody came ; and, at two, the exhausted family sat down in a blaze of sunshine to consume the perishable portions of the feast, that nothing might be lost.

" No doubt about the weather to-day ; they will certainly come, so we must fly round and be ready for them," said Amy, as the sun woke her next morning.

" I can't get any lobsters, so you will have to do without salad to-day," said Mr. March, coming in half an hour later, with an expression of placid despair.

" Use the chicken then, the toughness won't matter in a salad," advised his wife.

" Hannah left it on the kitchen table a minute, and the kittens got at it. I'm very sorry, Amy," added Beth, who was still a patroness of cats.

" Then, I *must* have a lobster, for tongue alone won't do," said Amy, decidedly.

" Shall I rush into town and demand one ? " asked Jo, with the magnanimity of a martyr.

" You'd come bringing it home under your arm, without any paper, just to try me. I'll go myself," answered Amy, whose temper was beginning to fail.

After some delay, the object of her desire was procured, likewise a bottle of dressing, to prevent further loss of time at home, and off she drove again, well pleased with her own forethought.

As the omnibus contained only one other passenger, a sleepy old lady, Amy pocketed her veil, and beguiled the tedium of the way by trying to find out where all her money had gone to. So busy was she with her card full of refractory figures that she did not observe a newcomer who entered, till a masculine voice said, " Good-morning, Miss March," and looking up she beheld one of Laurie's most elegant college friends. Fervently hoping that he would get out before she did, Amy utterly ignored the basket at her feet, and congratulating herself that she had on her new travelling dress, returned the young man's greeting with her usual suavity and spirit.

They got on excellently ; for Amy's chief care was soon set at rest, by learning that the gentleman would leave first, and she was chatting away in a peculiarly lofty strain, when the old lady got out. In stumbling to the door, she upset the basket, and oh, horror! the lobster, in all its vulgar size and brilliancy, was revealed to the high-born eyes of a Tudor!

"By Jove, she's forgot her dinner!" cried the unconscious youth, poking the scarlet monster into its place with his cane, and preparing to hand the basket after the old lady.

"Please don't—it's—it's mine," murmured Amy, with a face nearly as red as her fish.

"Oh, really, I beg pardon; it's an uncommonly fine one, isn't it?" said Tudor, with great presence of mind, and an air of sober interest that did credit to his breeding.

Amy recovered herself in a breath, set her basket boldly on the seat, and said, laughing—

"Don't you wish you were to have some of the salad he's to make, and to see the charming young ladies who are to eat it?"

Now that was tact, for two of the ruling foibles of the masculine mind were touched; the lobster was instantly surrounded by a halo of pleasing reminiscences, and curiosity about "the charming young ladies" diverted his mind from the comical mishap.

"I suppose he'll laugh and joke over it with Laurie, but I shan't see them; that's a comfort," thought Amy, as Tudor bowed and departed.

Feeling that the neighbours were interested in her movements, she wished to efface the memory of yesterday's failure by a grand success to-day; so she ordered the "cherry-bounce," and drove away in state to meet and escort her guests to the banquet.

"There's the rumble, they're coming! I'll go into the porch to meet them," said Mrs. March, suiting the action to the word. But after one glance, she retired with an indescribable expression, for, looking quite lost in the big carriage, sat Amy and one young lady.

"Run, Beth, and help Hannah clear half the things off the table; it will be too absurd to put a luncheon for twelve before a single girl," cried Jo, hurrying away.

In came Amy, quite calm, and delightfully cordial to the one guest who had kept her promise; the rest of the family, being of a dramatic turn, played their parts equally well, and Miss Eliott found them a most hilarious set ; for it was impossible to entirely control the merriment which possessed them. The remodelled lunch being gaily partaken of, the studio and garden visited, and art discussed with enthusiasm, Amy ordered a buggy (alas for the elegant cherry-bounce !) and drove her friend quietly about the neighbourhood till sunset, when "the party went out."

As she came walking in, looking very tired, but as composed as ever, she observed that every vestige of the unfortunate fête had disappeared, except a suspicious pucker about the corners of Jo's mouth.

" You've had a lovely afternoon for your drive, dear," said her mother, as respectfully as if the whole twelve had come.

" Miss Eliott is a very sweet girl, and seemed to enjoy herself, I thought," observed Beth, with unusual warmth.

" It's a pity Laurie isn't here to help us," began Jo, as they sat down to ice-cream and salad for the fourth time in two days.

A warning look from her mother checked any further remarks, and the whole family ate in heroic silence, till Mr. March mildly observed, " Salad was one of the favourite dishes of the ancients, and Evelyn "—here a general explosion of laughter cut short the " history of sallets," to the great surprise of the learned gentleman.

" Bundle everything into a basket and send it to the Hummels. I'm sick of the sight of this ; and there's no reason you should all die of a surfeit because I've been a fool," cried Amy, wiping her eyes.

" I'm very sorry you were disappointed, dear, but we all did our best to satisfy you," said Mrs. March, in a tone full of motherly regret.

" I *am* satisfied ; I've done what I undertook, and it's not my fault that it failed " ; said Amy, with a little quiver in her voice. " I thank you all very much for helping me, and I'll thank you still more, if you won't allude to it for a month, at least."

No one did for several months ; but Laurie's birthday gift to Amy was a tiny coral lobster in the shape of a charm for her watchguard.

CHAPTER IV

LITERARY LESSONS

FORTUNE suddenly smiled upon Jo, and dropped a good-luck penny in her path. Every few weeks she would shut herself up in her room, put on her scribbling suit, and "fall into a vortex," as she expressed it, writing away at her novel with all her heart and soul, for till that was finished she could find no peace. Her "scribbling suit" consisted of a black pinafore on which she could wipe her pen at will, and a cap of the same material, adorned with a cheerful red bow, into which she bundled her hair when the decks were cleared for action. This cap was a beacon to the inquiring eyes of her family, who, during these periods, kept their distance, merely popping in their heads semi-occasionally, to ask, with interest, " Does genius burn, Jo ? " They did not always venture even to ask this question, but took an observation of the cap, and judged accordingly. If this expressive article of dress was drawn low upon the forehead, it was a sign that hard work was going on ; in exciting moments it was pushed rakishly askew, and when despair seized the author it was plucked wholly off, and cast upon the floor. At such times the intruder silently withdrew ; and not until the red bow was seen gaily erect upon the gifted brow, did anyone dare address Jo.

She did not think herself a genius by any means ; but when the writing fit came on, she gave herself up to it with entire abandon. Sleep forsook her eyes, meals stood untasted, day and night were all too short to enjoy the happiness which made these hours worth living, even if they bore no other fruit.

She was just recovering from one of these attacks when she was prevailed upon to escort Miss Crocker to a lecture on " The Pyramids of Egypt." They were early ; and Jo amused herself by examining the faces of the people who occupied the seat with them. On her left were two matrons discussing Woman's Rights and making tatting. On her right, her only neighbour was a studious-looking lad absorbed in a newspaper.

It was a pictorial sheet, and Jo examined the work of art nearest her, idly wondering what circumstances needed the melodramatic illustration of an Indian in full war costume, tumbling over a precipice with a wolf at his throat, while a dishevelled female was flying away in the background. Pausing to turn a page, the lad saw her looking, and, with boyish good-nature, offered half his paper, saying, bluntly, " Want to read it ? That's a first-rate story."

Jo accepted it with a smile, for she had never outgrown her liking for lads, and soon found herself involved in the usual labyrinth of love, mystery, and murder.

" Prime, isn't it ? " asked the boy, as her eye went down the last paragraph of her portion.

" I guess you and I could do most as well as that if we tried," returned Jo, amused at his admiration of the trash.

" I should think I was a pretty lucky chap if I could. She makes a good living out of such stories, they say " ; and he pointed to the name of Mrs. S. Northbury, under the title of the tale.

" Do you know her ? " asked Jo, with sudden interest.

" No ; but I read all her pieces, and I know a fellow that works in the office where this paper is printed."

" Do you say she makes a good living out of stories like this ? " and Jo looked more respectfully at the paper.

" Guess she does ! she knows just what folks like, and gets paid well for writing it."

Here the lecture began, but Jo heard very little of it, for while Professor Sands was prosing away about scarabei, and hieroglyphics, she was covertly taking down the address of the paper, and boldly resolving to try for the hundred dollar prize offered in its columns for a sensational story. By the time the lecture ended, she was already deep in the concoction of her story, being unable to decide whether the duel should come before the elopement or after the murder.

She said nothing of her plan at home, but fell to work next day, much to the disquiet of her mother, who always looked a little anxious when " genius took to burning." Her story was as full of desperation and despair as her limited acquaintance with those uncomfortable emotions enabled her to make it, and, having located it in Lisbon, she wound up with an earthquake, as a striking and appropriate *dénouement*.

Six weeks is a long time to wait, and a still longer time for a girl to keep a secret ; but Jo did both, and was just beginning to give up all hope of ever seeing her manuscript again, when a letter arrived which almost took her breath away ; for, on opening it, a cheque for a hundred dollars fell into her lap. For a minute she stared at it, then she read her letter, and began to cry.

A prouder young woman was seldom seen than when, having composed herself, she electrified the family by appearing before them with the letter in one hand, the cheque in the other, announcing that she had won the prize ! Of course there was a great jubilee, and when the story came every one read and praised it.

" What *will* you do with such a fortune ? " asked Amy. regarding the magic slip of paper with a reverential eye,

" Send Beth and mother to the seaside for a month or two," answered Jo promptly.

" Oh, how splendid ! No, I can't do it, dear, it would be so selfish," cried Beth, who had clapped her thin hands, then stopped herself.

" Ah, but you shall go, I've set my heart on it ; that's what I tried for, and that's why I succeeded. I never get on when I think of myself alone, so it will help me to work for you, don't you see."

To the seaside they went, after much discussion ; and Beth returned much better, while Mrs. March declared she felt ten years younger ; so Jo was satisfied with the investment of her prize-money, and fell to work with a cheery spirit, bent on earning more of those delightful cheques. She did earn several that year, and began to feel herself a power in the house ; for by the magic of a pen, her " rubbish " turned into comforts for them all. *The Duke's Daughter* paid the butcher's bill, *A Phantom Hand* put down a new carpet, and *The Curse of the Coventrys* proved the blessing of the Marches in the way of groceries and gowns. Encouraged by these small successes, Jo resolved to make a bold stroke for fame and fortune. Having copied her novel for the fourth time, and submitted it with fear and trembling to three publishers, she at last disposed of it, on condition that she would cut it down one-third, and omit all the parts which she particularly admired.

"Fame is a very good thing to have in the house, but cash is more convenient; so I wish to take the sense of the meeting on this important subject," said Jo, calling a family council.

"Don't spoil your book, my girl, for there is more in it than you know, and the idea is well worked out. Let it wait and ripen," was her father's advice.

"It seems to me that Jo will profit more by making the trial than by waiting," said Mrs. March. "We are too partial; but the praise and blame of outsiders will prove useful, even if she gets but little money."

"Yes," said Jo, knitting her brows, "that's just it; I've been fussing over the thing so long, I really don't know whether it's good, bad, or indifferent. It will be a great help to have cool, impartial persons tell me what they think of it."

"I wouldn't leave out a word of it; you'll spoil it if you do," said Meg, who firmly believed that this book was the most remarkable novel ever written.

"But Mr. Allen says, 'Leave out the explanations, make it brief and dramatic, and let the characters tell the story,'" interrupted Jo, turning to the publisher's note.

"Do as he tells you; he knows what will sell, and we don't. By-and-by, when you've got a name, you can afford to have philosophical people in your novels," said Amy, who took a strictly practical view of the subject.

"Well," said Jo, laughing, "Beth, what do you say?"

"I should like to see it printed *soon*," was all Beth said, and smiled in saying it; but there was a wistful look in her eyes which chilled Jo's heart with a foreboding fear, and decided her to make her little venture "soon."

So, with Spartan firmness, the young authoress laid her first-born on her table, and chopped it up as ruthlessly as any ogre. In the hope of pleasing everyone, she took everyone's advice; and, like the old man and his donkey in the fable, suited nobody. To complete the ruin, she cut it down one-third, and confidingly sent the poor little romance out into the big world, to try its fate.

Well, it was printed, and she got three hundred dollars

for it ; likewise plenty of praise and blame, from which
it took her some time to recover.

" You said, mother, that criticism would help me ; but
how can it, when I don't know whether I have written
a promising book, or broken all the ten commandments,"
cried poor Jo, turning over a heap of notices, the perusal
of which filled her with pride one minute, and dire dismay
the next. " Some make fun of it, some overpraise, and
nearly all insist that I had a deep theory to expound,
when I only wrote it for the pleasure and the money. I
wish I'd printed it whole, or not at all, for I do hate to be
so horridly misjudged."

Her family and friends administered comfort and
commendation liberally ; yet it was a hard time for sensitive
high-spirited Jo, who meant so well, and had apparently
done so ill.

" Not being a genius, like Keats, it won't kill me," she
said stoutly ; " and I've got the joke on my side, after
all ; for the parts that were taken straight out of real life,
are denounced as impossible, and the scenes that I made up
out of my own head, are pronounced ' charmingly natural.'
So I'll comfort myself with that and, when I'm ready,
I'll up again and take another."

CHAPTER V

DOMESTIC EXPERIENCES

LIKE most other young matrons, Meg began her married
life with the determination to be a model housekeeper.
John should find home a paradise ; he should always
see a smiling face, should fare sumptuously every day,
and never know the loss of a button. She brought so much
love, energy, and cheerfulness to the work, that she
could not but succeed in spite of some obstacles. They
were very happy even after they discovered that they
couldn't live on love alone. The little house ceased to
be a glorified bower, but it became a home, and the young
couple soon felt that it was a change for the better.

While the cooking mania lasted, she went through

Mrs. Cornelius's Receipt Book as if it were a mathematical exercise, working out the problems with patience and care. Sometimes her family were invited in to help eat up a too bounteous feast of successes, or Lotty would be privately despatched with a batch of failures which were to be concealed from all eyes, in the convenient stomachs of the little Hummels. An evening with John over the account books usually produced a temporary lull in the culinary enthusiasm, and a frugal fit would ensue, during which the poor man was put through a course of bread pudding, hash, and warmed-over coffee, which tried his soul, although he bore it with praiseworthy fortitude. Before the golden mean was found, however, Meg added to her domestic possessions what young couples seldom get on long without—a family jar.

Fired with a housewifely wish to see her store-room stocked with home-made preserves, she undertook to put up her own currant jelly. John was requested to order home a dozen or so of little pots, and an extra quantity of sugar, for their own currants were ripe, and were to be attended to at once. As John firmly believed that " my wife " was equal to anything, home came four dozen little pots, half a barrel of sugar, and a small boy to pick the currants for her. With her pretty hair tucked into a little cap and a checked apron, which had a coquettish look in spite of the bib, the young housewife fell to work, feeling no doubt about her success ; for hadn't she seen Hannah do it hundreds of times ? She spent a long day picking, boiling, straining, and fussing over her jelly, but that dreadful stuff wouldn't " *jell*."

She longed to run home, and ask mother to lend a hand, but John and she had agreed that they would never annoy anyone with their private worries, experiments, or quarrels. They had laughed over that last word as if the idea it suggested was a most preposterous one ; but they had held to their resolve and no one interfered—for Mrs. March had advised the plan. So Meg wrestled alone with the refractory sweetmeats all that hot summer day, and at five o'clock sat down in her topsy-turvy kitchen and wept.

Now in the first flush of the new life, she had often said— " John, dear, never stop to ask my leave, invite whom you please, and be sure of a welcome from me."

How charming that was, to be sure ! John quite glowed

with pride to hear her say it. If he had not forgotten all about the jelly, it really would have been unpardonable in him to choose that day, of all the days in the year, to bring a friend home to dinner unexpectedly. Congratulating himself that a handsome repast had been ordered that morning, and indulging in pleasant anticipations of the charming effect it would produce, when his pretty wife came running out to meet him, he escorted his friend to his mansion, with the irrepressible satisfaction of a young host and husband.

It is a world of disappointments, as John discovered when he reached the Dovecote. No bright-eyed hostess appeared, smiling a shy welcome as she greeted her guest; only a sanguinary-looking boy asleep under the currant bushes.

"I'm afraid something has happened; step into the garden, Scott, while I look up Mrs. Brooke," said John, alarmed at the silence.

Round the house he hurried and Mr. Scott strolled after him. He paused discreetly at a distance when Brooke disappeared, but could both see and hear, and, being a bachelor, enjoyed the prospect mightily.

In the kitchen reigned confusion and despair, jelly trickled from pot to floor, and Lotty was calmly eating bread and currant wine while Mrs. Brooke, with her apron over her head, sat sobbing dismally.

"My dearest girl, what is the matter?" cried John, rushing in with awful visions of scalded hands and consternation at the thought of the guest in the garden.

"Oh, John, I *am* so tired, and hot, and cross, and worried! Do come and help me, or I *shall* die"; and the exhausted housewife cast herself upon his breast, giving him a sweet welcome in every sense of the word, for her pinafore had been baptised at the same time as the floor.

Has anything dreadful happened?" asked the anxious John, tenderly kissing the crown of the little cap, which was all askew.

"Tell me quick, then; don't cry, I can bear anything better than that."

"The—the jelly won't jell—and I don't know what to do!"

John Brooke laughed then as he never dared to laugh afterward; and the derisive Scott smiled involuntarily as he heard the hearty peal, which put the finishing stroke to poor Meg's woe.

" Is that all ? Fling it out of the window. I'll buy you quarts if you want it ; but for heaven's sake don't have hysterics, for I've brought Jack Scott home to dinner, and——"

John got no further, for Meg cast him off, and clasped her hands with a tragic gesture as she fell into a chair, exclaiming in a tone of mingled indignation and dismay—

" A man to dinner, and everything in a mess ! John Brooke, how *could* you do such a thing ? "

" I never thought of asking leave, when you have always told me to do as I liked," said John, with an aggrieved air.

He restrained himself, however, and the little squall would have blown over but for one unlucky word.

" Don't cry, dear, but just knock us up something to eat. Give us the cold meat, and bread and cheese ; we won't ask for jelly."

He meant it for a good-natured joke ; but Meg thought it was *too* cruel to hint about her sad failure, and the last atom of patience vanished as he spoke.

" It's like a man, to propose a bone and vulgar bread and cheese for company. I won't have anything of the sort in my house. Take that Scott up to mother's, and tell him I'm away—sick, dead, anything. I won't see him, and you two can laugh at me and my jelly as much as you like ! " Meg cast away her pinafore, and precipitately left the field to bemoan herself in her own room.

What those two creatures did in her absence, she never knew ; but when Meg descended, after they had strolled away together, she found traces of a promiscuous lunch which filled her with horror. Lotty reported that they had eaten " a much, and greatly laughed."

Meg longed to go and tell mother ; but a sense of shame at her own short-comings, of loyalty to John restrained her ; and after a summary clearing up, she dressed herself prettily, and sat down to wait for John to come and be forgiven.

Unfortunately, John didn't come, not seeing the matter in that light. He had carried it off as a good joke with Scott, excused his little wife as well as he could, and played the host so hospitably, that his friend enjoyed the

impromptu dinner, and promised to come again. But
John was angry, though he did not show it ; he felt that
Meg had got him into a scrape, and then deserted him in
his hour of need. She was wrong, of course, but then she
was young. "I must be patient, and teach her," he
thought. He hoped she had not gone home, and then
the fear that Meg would cry herself sick sent him on at a
quicker pace, resolving to be kind, but firm, and show
her where she had failed in her duty to her spouse.

Meg likewise resolved to be "calm and kind, but firm,"
and show *him* his duty.

John, feeling that his dignity demanded the first apology
came leisurely in, and laid himself upon the sofa, with the
singularly relevant remark—

"We are going to have a new moon, my dear."

"I've no objection," was Meg's equally soothing remark.

A few other topics of general interest were introduced
by Mr. Brooke, and wet-blanketed by Mrs. Brooke, and
conversation languished. Neither spoke—both looked
quite "calm and firm," and both felt desperately
uncomfortable.

"Oh, dear," thought Meg, "married life is very trying,
and does need infinite patience, as well as love, as mother
says." The word "mother" suggested other maternal
counsels given long ago, and received with unbelieving
protests.

"John is a good man, but he has his faults, and you
must learn to see and bear with them, remembering your
own. He has a temper, not like ours—one flash, and then
all over—but the white still anger that is seldom stirred,
but once kindled is hard to quench. Watch yourself,
be the first to ask pardon if you both err, and guard against
the little misunderstandings, and hasty words that often
pave the way for bitter sorrow and regret."

These words came back to Meg as she sat sewing in the
sunset, especially the last. She glanced at him with tears
in her eyes, but he did not see them ; she went very slowly
across the room and stooping down she softly kissed her
husband on the forehead. Of course, that settled it ;
the penitent kiss was better than a world of words ,and John
had her on his knee in a minute, saying tenderly—

"It was too bad to laugh at the poor little jelly-pots ;
forgive me, dear, I never will again !"

" The—the jelly won't jell . . . "

[*see page* 30

But he did, hundreds of times, and so did Meg, both declaring that it was the sweetest jelly they ever made ; for family peace was preserved in that little family jar.

After this, Meg had Mr. Scott to dinner by special invitation, and served him up a pleasant feast without a cooked wife for the first course ; on which occasion she was so gay and gracious, and made everything go off so charmingly, that Mr. Scott told John he was a happy fellow, and shook his head over the hardships of bachelorhood all the way home.

In the autumn, new trials and experiences came to Meg. Sallie Moffat renewed her friendship, was always running out for a dish of gossip at the little house, or inviting " that poor dear " to come in and spend the day at the big house. Seeing Sallie's pretty things made her long for such, and pity herself because she had not got them.

She knew her husband's income, and she loved to feel that he trusted her, not only with his happiness, but what some men seem to value more, his money. Till now she had done well, been prudent and exact, kept her little account-books neatly, and showed them to him monthly without fear. But Meg didn't like to be pitied and made to feel poor ; and now and then she tried to console herself by buying something pretty, so that Sallie needn't think she had to scrimp. They cost so little it wasn't worth worrying about ; so the trifles increased unconsciously, and in the shopping excursions she was no longer a passive looker-on.

But a few days before she had done a dreadful thing, and it weighed upon her conscience. Sally had been buying silks, and Meg ached for a new one. Aunt March usually gave the sisters a present of twenty-five dollars a-piece, at New Year ; that was only a month to wait, and here was a lovely violet silk going at a bargain, and she had the money, if only she dared to take it. Sallie had urged her to do it, had offered to loan the money, and with the best intentions in life, had tempted Meg beyond her strength. In an evil moment the shopman held up the lovely, shimmering folds, and said, " A bargain, I assure you, ma'am." She answered, " I'll take it ; " and it was cut off and paid for, and Sallie had exulted, and she had driven away feeling as if she had stolen something, and the police were after her.

c

When John got out his books that night, Meg's heart sank ; and, for the first time in her married life, she was afraid of her husband. The kind, brown eyes looked as if they could be stern ; and though he was unusually merry, she fancied he had found her out, but didn't mean to let her know it. The house bills were all paid, the books all in order. John had praised her, and was undoing the old pocket-book which they called the " bank," when Meg, knowing that it was quite empty, stopped his hand, saying nervously,—

" You haven't seen my private expense book, yet."

John had never asked to see it ; but she always insisted on his doing so, and used to enjoy his masculine amazement at the queer things women wanted, and make him guess what piping was.

The little book was brought slowly out, and laid down before him. Meg got behind his chair, under pretence of smoothing the wrinkles out of his tired forehead, and standing there, she said, with her panic increasing with every word,—

" John, dear, I'm ashamed to show you my book, for I've really been dreadfully extravagant lately. I go about so much I must have things, you know, and Sallie advised my getting it, so I did ; and my New-Year's money will partly pay for it ; but I was sorry after I'd done it, for I knew you'd think it wrong of me."

John laughed, and drew her round beside him, saying, good-humouredly, " Don't go and hide, I won't beat you if you *have* got a pair of killing boots ; I'm rather proud of my wife's feet."

That had been one of her last " trifles," and John's eye had fallen on it as he spoke. " Oh, what *will* he say when he comes to that awful fifty dollars ! " thought Meg, with a shiver.

" It's worse than boots, it's a silk dress," she said, with the calmness of desperation, for she wanted the worst over.

She turned the page and her head at the same time, pointing to the sum. For a minute the room was very still ; then John said, slowly but she could feel it cost him an effort to express no displeasure,—

" Twenty yards of silk seems a good deal to cover one small woman, but I've no doubt my wife will look as fine as Ned Moffat's when she gets it on," said John dryly.

"I know you are angry, John, but I didn't think those little things would count up so. I can't resist them when I see Sallie buying all she wants, and pitying me because I don't; I try to be contented, but I'm tired of being poor."

She could have bitten her tongue out the minute she had said it, for John pushed the books away and got up, saying, with a little quiver in his voice, "I was afraid of this; I do my best, Meg." She ran to him and held him close, crying, with repentant tears, "Oh, John! my dear, kind, hard-working boy, I didn't mean it! Oh, how could I say it!"

He was very kind, forgave her readily, and did not utter one reproach; but Meg knew that she had done and said a thing which would not be forgotten soon, although he might never allude to it again. It was dreadful; and the worst of it was John went on so quietly afterward, just as if nothing had happened, except that he stayed in town later, and worked at night when she had gone to cry herself to sleep. The discovery that he had countermanded the order for his new greatcoat, reduced her to a state of despair which was pathetic to behold. He had simply said, in answer to her surprised inquiries as to the change, "I can't afford it, my dear."

Meg said no more, but a few minutes after he found her in the hall with her face buried in the old great-coat, crying as if her heart would break.

They had a long talk that night, and Meg learned to love her husband better for his poverty, because it seemed to have made a man of him—giving him the strength and courage to fight his own way—and taught him a tender patience with which to bear and comfort the natural longings and failures of those he loved.

Next day she put her pride in her pocket, went to Sallie, told the truth, and asked her to buy the silk as a favour. The good-natured Mrs. Moffat willingly did so, and had the delicacy not to make her a present of it immediately afterward. Then Meg ordered home the great coat, and when John arrived, she put it on, and asked him how he liked her new silk gown. One can imagine what answer he made, how he received his present, and what a blissful state of things ensued. John came home early, Meg gadded no more; and that great-coat was put on in the morning by a very happy husband, and taken off at night by a most devoted little wife. So the year rolled round, and at midsummer there came to Meg a new experience,—the deepest and tenderest of a woman's life.

Laurie came creeping into the kitchen of the Dovecote one Saturday, with an excited face, and was received with the clash of cymbals; for Hannah clapped her hands with a saucepan in one, and the cover in the other.

"How's the little Ma? Where is everybody? Why didn't you tell me before I came home?" began Laurie, in a loud whisper.

"Happy as a queen, the dear! Every soul of 'em is upstairs a worshippin'. Now you go into the parlour, and I'll send 'em down to you," with which Hannah vanished, chuckling ecstatically.

Presently Jo appeared, proudly bearing a small flannel bundle laid forth upon a large pillow.

"Shut your eyes and hold out your arms," she said invitingly.

Laurie backed into a corner, and put his hands behind him with an imploring gesture,—"No, thank you. I shall drop it, as sure as fate."

"Then you shan't see your nevvy," said Jo, turning as if to go.

"I will, I will! only you must be responsible for damages"; and Laurie heroically shut his eyes while something was put into his arms. A peal of laughter from Jo caused him to open them to find himself invested with two babies instead of one.

No wonder they laughed, for the expression of his face was droll enough to convulse a Quaker, as he stared wildly from the unconscious innocents to the hilarious spectators.

"Twins, by Jupiter!" was all he said for a minute; then turning to the women with an appealing look he added, "Take 'em quick, somebody! I'm going to laugh, and drop 'em."

John rescued his babies, and marched up and down, with one on each arm while Laurie laughed till the tears ran down his cheeks.

"It's the best joke of the season, isn't it? I wouldn't have you told, for I set my heart on surprising you," said Jo.

"I never was more staggered in my life. Are they boys? Hold me up, Jo; it's one too many for me," returned Laurie.

regarding the infants with the air of a big Newfoundland looking at a pair of infantile kittens.

" Boy and girl. Aren't they beauties ? " said the proud papa, beaming upon the little, red squirmers.

" Most remarkable children I ever saw. Which is which ? " and Laurie bent to examine the prodigies.

" Amy put a blue ribbon on the boy and a pink on the girl, French fashion, so you can always tell. Besides, one has blue eyes and one brown. Kiss them, Uncle Teddy," said wicked Jo.

Laurie obeyed with a gingerly peck at each little cheek that made the babies squeal.

" There, I knew they didn't like it ! That's the boy ; see him kick ! Now then, young Brooke, pitch into a man of your own size, will you ? " cried Laurie, delighted with a poke in the face from a tiny fist.

" He's to be named John Laurence, and the girl Margaret, after mother and grandmother. We shall call her Daisy, so as not to have two Megs, and I suppose the mannie will be Jack, unless we find a better name," said Amy, with aunt-like interest.

" Name him Demijohn, and call him ' Demi ' for short," said Laurie.

" Daisy and Demi,—just the thing ! I *knew* Teddy would do it," cried Jo, clapping her hands.

Teddy certainly had done it that time, for the babies were " Daisy " and " Demi " to the end of the chapter.

CHAPTER VI

CALLS

" Come, Jo, it's time."

" For what ? "

" You don't mean to say you have forgotten that you promised to make half-a-dozen calls with me to-day ? "

" I've done a good many rash and foolish things in my

life, but I don't think I ever was mad enough to say I'd make six calls in one day, when a single one upsets me for a week."

" Yes, you did ; it was a bargain between us. I was to finish the crayon of Beth for you, and you were to go properly with me, and return our neighbours' visits."

" If it was fair—that was in the bond ; and I stand to the letter of my bond, Shylock. There is a pile of clouds in the east ; it's not *fair*, and I don't go."

" Now that's shirking," cried Amy. " It's a lovely day, no prospect of rain, and you pride yourself on keeping promises ; so be honourable. You can talk so well, and behave so beautifully, if you try, that I'm proud of you. I'm afraid to go alone ; do come and take care of me."

" You're an artful little puss to flatter and wheedle your cross old sister in that way. Well, I'll go if I must, and do my best ; you shall be commander of the expedition, and I'll obey blindly ; will that satisfy you ? " said Jo, with a sudden change from perversity to lamb-like submission.

" You're a perfect cherub ! Now put on all your best things, and I'll tell you how to behave at each place, so that you will make a good impression. I want people to like you, and they would if you'd only try to be a little more agreeable."

While Amy dressed, she issued her orders, and Jo sighed as she rustled into her new organdie, frowned darkly at herself as she tied her bonnet strings in an irreproachable bow, and when she had squeezed her hands into tight gloves with two buttons and a tassel, as the last touch of elegance, she turned to Amy with an imbecile expression of countenance, saying meekly,—

" I'm perfectly miserable ; but if you consider me presentable, I'll die happy."

" Turn slowly round, and let me get a careful view." Jo revolved, and Amy fell back with her head on one side, observing graciously, " Yes, you'll do. Hold back your shoulders, and carry your hands easily, no matter if your gloves do pinch. There's one thing you can do well, Jo ; that is, wear a shawl, and I'm so glad Aunt March gave you that lovely one. Is the point of my mantle in the middle, and have I looped my dress evenly ? "

" You are a thing of beauty, and a joy for ever," said
Jo, looking at the golden hair. " Am I to drag my best
dress through the dust, or loop it up, please ma'am ? "

" Hold it up when you walk, but drop it in the house ;
the sweeping style suits you best, and you must learn to
trail your skirts gracefully. Now, Jo dear, the Chesters are
very elegant people, so I want you to put on your best
deportment. Don't make any of your abrupt remarks.
or do anything odd, will you ? Just be calm, cool and
quiet,—that's safe and lady-like ; and you can easily do it
for fifteen minutes."

" Let me see ; ' Calm, cool and quiet ! ' yes, I think I
can promise that."

Amy looked relieved, but naughty Jo took her at her
word ; for, during the first call, she sat with every limb
gracefully composed, every fold correctly draped, calm as
a summer sea, cool as a snow-bank, and as silent as a
sphinx. In vain Mrs. Chester alluded to her " charming
novel," and the Misses Chester introduced parties, pic-nics,
the Opera and the fashions ; each and all were answered
by a smile, a bow, and a demure " Yes " or " No," with
the chill on.

" What a haughty, uninteresting creature that oldest Miss
March is ! " was the unfortunately audible remark of one
of the ladies, as the door closed upon their guests. Jo
laughed noiselessly all through the hall, but Amy looked
disgusted at the failure of her instructions, and very
naturally laid the blame upon Jo.

" How could you mistake me so ? I merely meant you
to be properly dignified and composed, and you made yourself a perfect stock and stone. Try to be sociable at the
Lambs ; gossip as other girls do, and be interested in dress,
and flirtations, and whatever nonsense comes up."

" I'll be agreeable ; I'll gossip and giggle, and have
horrors and raptures over any trifle you like. See if the
Lambs don't say, ' What a lively, nice creature that Jo
March is ! ' "

Amy felt anxious, as well she might, for when Jo turned
freakish there was no knowing where she would stop. Amy's
face was a study when she saw her sister skim into the next
drawing-room, kiss all the young ladies with effusion, beam
graciously upon the young gentlemen, and join in the chat
with a spirit which amazed the beholder. One may

imagine her suffering on overhearing fragments of this sort
of conversation :

" She rides splendidly,—who taught her ? "

" No one; she used to practise mounting, holding the
reins, and sitting straight on an old saddle in a tree. Now
she rides anything and the stable-man lets her have
horses cheap, because she trains them to carry ladies so
well."

At this speech Amy contained herself with difficulty, for
the impression was being given that she was rather a fast
young lady, which was her especial aversion. But what
could she do ? One of the young ladies asked Jo where she
got the pretty drab hat she wore to the picnic ; and stupid
Jo, instead of mentioning the place where it was bought two
years ago, must needs answer, with unnecessary frankness,
" Oh, Amy painted it ; you can't buy those soft shades,
so we paint ours any colour we like. It's a great comfort
to have an artistic sister."

" Isn't that an original idea ? " cried Miss Lamb, who
found Jo great fun.

" That's nothing compared to some of her brilliant performances. There's nothing the child can't do. Why, she
wanted a pair of blue boots for Sallie's party, so she just
painted her soiled white ones the loveliest shade of sky-blue
you ever saw, and they looked exactly like satin," added
Jo with an air of pride in her sister's accomplishments that
exasperated Amy till she felt that it would be a relief to
throw her card-case at her.

" We read a story of yours the other day, and enjoyed it
very much," observed the elder Miss Lamb, wishing to
compliment the literary lady, who did not look the character
just then, it must be confessed. Any mention of her
" works " always had a bad effect upon Jo, who either grew
rigid, and looked offended, or changed the subject with a
brusque remark, as now. " Sorry you could find nothing
better to read. I write that rubbish because it sells, and
ordinary people like it. Are you going to New York this
winter ? "

As Miss Lamb had " enjoyed " the story, this speech was
not exactly grateful or complimentary. The minute it was
made, Jo saw her mistake, but fearing to make the matter
worse, suddenly remembered that it was for her to make
the first move towards departure, and did so with an abrupt-

ness that left three people with half-finished sentences in their mouths.

"Amy, we *must* go. *Good*-bye, dear; *do* come and see us; we are *pining* for a visit."

Jo said this with such a droll imitation of May Chester's gushing style, that Amy got out of the room as rapidly as possible, feeling a strong desire to laugh and cry at the same time.

"Didn't I do that well?" asked Jo, with a satisfied air, as they walked away.

"Nothing could have been worse," was Amy's crushing reply. "You needn't go and tell them all our little shifts, and expose our poverty in that perfectly unnecessary way. You haven't a bit of proper pride, and never will learn when to hold your tongue, and when to speak," said Amy despairingly.

"How shall I behave here?" asked poor Jo, as they approached the third mansion.

"Just as you please; I wash my hands of you," was Amy's short answer.

"Then I'll enjoy myself. The boys are at home, and we'll have a comfortable time," returned Jo, disturbed by her failures to suit.

An enthusiastic welcome from three big boys and several pretty children, speedily soothed her ruffled feelings; and, leaving Amy to entertain the hostess and Mr. Tudor, who happened to be calling likewise, Jo devoted herself to the young folks, and found the change refreshing.

Leaving her sister to her own devices, Amy proceeded to enjoy herself to her heart's content. Mr. Tudor's uncle had married an English lady who was third cousin to a living lord, and Amy regarded the whole family with great respect. But even the satisfaction of talking with a distant connection of the British nobility did not render Amy forgetful of time; and, when the proper number of minutes had passed, she reluctantly tore herself from this aristo-cratic society and looked about for Jo,—fervently hoping that her incorrigible sister would not be found in any position which should bring disgrace upon the name of March.

It might have been worse; but Amy considered it bad, for Jo sat on the grass with an encampment of boys about her, and a dirty-footed dog reposing on the skirt of her state and festival dress, as she related one of Laurie's pranks to her admiring audience.

" Capital boys, aren't they ? " said Jo, strolling along with her hands behind her.

" Why do you always avoid Mr. Tudor ? " asked Amy, wisely refraining from any comment upon Jo's appearance.

" Don't like him ; he puts on airs, snubs his sisters, worries his father, and doesn't speak respectfully of his mother."

" You might treat him civilly at least. You gave him a cool nod ; and bowed and smiled in the politest way to Tommy Chamberlain, whose father keeps a grocery store. If you had just reversed the nod and the bow, it would have been right," said Amy, reprovingly.

" No it wouldn't," returned perverse Jo; " I neither respect not admire Tudor, though his grandfather's uncle's nephew's niece *was* third cousin to a lord. Tommy is poor, and bashful, and very clever ; I think well of him, and like to show that I do, for he *is* a gentleman in spite of the brown paper parcels."

" It's no use trying to argue with you," began Amy.

" Not the least, my dear," cut in Jo ; " so let us go home, and never mind Aunt March to-day. We can run down there any time, and it's really a pity to trail through the dust in our best bibs and tuckers, when we are tired and cross."

" Speak for yourself, if you please ; aunt likes to have us pay her the compliment of coming in style, and making a formal call; it's a little thing to do, but it gives her pleasure and I don't believe it will hurt your things half so much as letting dirty dogs and clumping boys spoil them."

" What a good girl you are, Amy," said Jo, with a repentant glance. " I wish it was as easy for me to do little things to please people, as it is for you. I wait for a chance to confer a big favour, and let the small ones slip ; but they tell best in the end, I guess."

Amy smiled, saying with a maternal air : " Women should learn to be agreeable, particularly poor ones ; for they have no other way of repaying the kindnesses they receive. Compose yourself now, and don't worry aunt with your new ideas."

" I'll try not to, but I'm always possessed to burst out

with some particularly blunt speech or revolutionary sentiment before her; it's my doom, and I can't help it."

They found Aunt Carrol with the old lady, both absorbed in some very interesting subject; but they dropped it as the girls came in, with a conscious look which betrayed that they had been talking about their nieces. Jo was not in a good humour, and the perverse fit returned; but Amy, who had virtuously done her duty, kept her temper, and pleased everybody, was in a most angelic frame of mind. This amiable spirit was felt at once, and both the aunts "my dear'd" her affectionately, looking what they afterwards said emphatically: "That child improves every day."

"Are you going to help about the fair, dear?" asked Mrs. Carrol, as Amy sat down beside her with the confiding air elderly people like so well in the young.

"Yes, aunt, Mrs. Chester asked me if I would, and I offered to tend a table, as I have nothing but my time to give."

"I'm not," put in Jo, decidedly; "I hate to be patronized, and the Chesters think it's a great favour to allow us to help with their highly connected fair. I wonder you consented, Amy—they only want you to work."

"I am willing to work,—it's for the Freedmen as well as the Chesters, and I think it very kind of them to let me share the labour and the fun."

"Quite right and proper; I like your grateful spirit, my dear; it's a pleasure to help people who appreciate our efforts," observed Aunt March, looking over her spectacles at Jo, who sat apart with a morose expression.

If Jo had only known what a great happiness was wavering in the balance for one of them, she would have turned dove-like in a minute; but, unfortunately, we cannot see what goes on in the minds of our friends. By her next speech, Jo deprived herself of several years of pleasure, and received a timely lesson in the art of holding her tongue.

"I don't like favours; they make me feel like a slave; I'd rather do everything for myself and be independent."

"Ahem!" coughed Aunt Carrol, with a look at Aunt March.

"I told you so," said Aunt March, with a nod to Aunt Carrol.

Mercifully unconscious of what she had done, Jo sat with her nose in the air, and a revolutionary aspect.

"Do you speak French, dear?" asked Mrs. Carrol, laying her hand on Amy's.

"Pretty well, thanks to Aunt March, who lets Esther talk to me as often as I like," replied Amy, with a grateful look, which caused the old lady to smile affably.

"Come and take a walk, my dear?" cried Polly, hopping toward the china-closet, with a look suggestive of lump-sugar.

"Thank you, I will—come, Amy," and Jo brought the visit to an end, feeling, more strongly than ever, that calls did have a bad effect upon her constitution. She shook hands in a gentlemanly manner, but Amy kissed both the Aunts, and the girls departed, leaving behind them the impression of shadow and sunshine; which impression caused Aunt March to say as they vanished:

"You'd better do it, Mary; I'll supply the money," and Aunt Carrol to reply, "I will, if her father and mother consent."

CHAPTER VII

CONSEQUENCES

MRS. CHESTER'S fair was so very elegant that it was considered a great honour by the young ladies of the neighbourhood to be invited to take a table. Amy was asked, but Jo was not, which was fortunate for all parties, as her elbows were decidedly akimbo at this period of her life, and it took a good many hard knocks to teach her how to get on easily.

Everything went on smoothly till the day before the fair opened; then there occurred one of the little skirmishes which it is almost impossible to avoid, when some five-and-twenty women, with all their private piques and prejudices try to work together.

May Chester was rather jealous of Amy because the latter was a greater favourite than herself; and several trifling circumstances occurred to increase the feeling. Amy's dainty pen-and-ink work entirely eclipsed May's painted vases ; that was one thorn ; then the all-conquering Tudor had danced four times with Amy at a late party, and only once with May ; that was thorn number two ; but the chief grievance was a rumour which some obliging gossip had whispered to her, that the March girls had made fun of her at the Lambs. No hint of this had reached the culprits, however, and Amy's dismay can be imagined when, the very late evening before the fair, Mrs. Chester, who, of course, resented the supposed ridicule of her daughter, said in a bland tone, but with a cold look—

" I find, dear, that there is some feeling among the young ladies about my giving this table to any one but my girls. I'm sorry, but I know you are too sincerely interested in the cause to mind a little personal disappointment, and you shall have another table if you like."

Amy felt that there was something behind this, but could not guess what, and said quietly—

" Perhaps you had rather I took no table at all ? "

" Now, my dear, don't have any ill feeling, I beg ; it's merely a matter of expediency, you see ; my girls will naturally take the lead, and this table is considered their proper place. Would you like the flower-table ? The little girls undertook it, but they are discouraged. You can make a charming thing of it, and the flower-table is always attractive, you know."

" Especially to gentlemen," added May, with a look which enlightened Amy as to one cause of her sudden fall from favour. She coloured angrily, but took no other notice of that girlish sarcasm, and answered with unexpected amiability—

" It shall be as you please, Mrs. Chester ; I'll give up my place here at once, and attend to the flowers if you like."

" You can put your own things on your own table, if you prefer," began May, feeling a little conscience-stricken, as she looked at the pretty racks, the painted shells, and quaint illuminations Amy had so carefully made. She meant it kindly, but Amy mistook her meaning, and said quickly—

" Oh, certainly, if they are in your way " ; and sweeping her contributions into her apron, she walked off, feeling that herself and her works of art had been insulted past forgiveness.

The little girls hailed Amy and her treasures with delight, which somewhat soothed her perturbed spirit, and she fell to work, determined so succeed florally, if she could not artistically. But everything seemed against her; it was late, and she was tired; every one was too busy with their own affairs to help her, and the little girls were only hindrances, making a great deal of confusion in their artless efforts to preserve the most perfect order. There was great indignation at home when she told her story that evening. Her mother said it was a shame, but told her she had done right. Beth declared she wouldn't go to the old fair at all, and Jo demanded why she didn't take all her pretty things and leave those mean people to get on without her.

"Because they are mean is no reason why I should be. I hate such things; and though I think I've a right to be hurt, I don't intend to show it. They will feel that more than angry speeches or huffy actions, won't they, Marmee?"

"That's the right spirit, my dear; a kiss for a blow is always best, though it's not very easy to give it, sometimes," said her mother, with the air of one who had learned the difference between preaching and practising.

In spite of various very natural temptations to resent and retaliate, Amy adhered to her resolution all the next day, bent on conquering her enemy by kindness.

A group of girls were standing about May's table, admiring the pretty things, and talking over the change of saleswomen. They dropped their voices, but Amy knew they were speaking of her, hearing one side of the story, and judging accordingly. It was not pleasant, but a better spirit had come over her and, presently she heard May say, sorrowfully—

"It's too bad, for there is no time to make other things. The table was just complete then—now it's spoilt."

"I dare say she'd put them back if you asked her," suggested some one.

"How could I, after all the fuss?" began May, but she did not finish, for Amy's voice came across the hall, saying pleasantly,—

"You may have them and welcome if you want them. I was just thinking I'd offer to put them back, for they belong to your table rather than mine. Please take them.

and forgive me if I was hasty in carrying them away last night."

As she spoke, Amy returned her contribution with a smile and hurried away again, feeling that it was easier to do a friendly thing than it was to stay and be thanked for it.

"Now I call that lovely of her, don't you?" cried one girl.

May's answer was inaudible; but another young lady, whose temper was evidently soured by making lemonade, added, with a laugh, "Very lovely; for she knew she wouldn't sell them at her own table."

Now that was hard; when we make little sacrifices we like to have them appreciated, at least; and for a minute Amy was sorry she had done it, feeling that virtue was not always its own reward. But it is—as she presently discovered; for her spirits began to rise, and her table to blossom under her skilful hands; the girls were very kind, and that one little act seemed to have cleared the atmosphere.

She did not go home till night, and then she looked so pale and quiet that they knew the day had been a hard one though she made no complaint, and did not even tell what she had done. Her mother gave her an extra cordial cup of tea, Beth helped her dress, and made a charming little wreath for her hair, while Jo astonished her family by getting herself up with unusual care, and hinting darkly that the tables were about to be turned.

"Don't do anything rude, pray, Jo; I won't have any fuss made, so let it all pass, and behave yourself," begged Amy, as she departed.

"I merely intend to make myself agreeable to everyone I know, and to keep them in your corner as long as possible. Teddy and his boys will lend a hand, and we'll have a good time yet," returned Jo, leaning over the gate to watch for Laurie. Presently the familiar tramp was heard in the dusk, and she ran out to meet him.

"Oh, Teddy, such doings!" and Jo told Amy's wrongs with sisterly zeal.

"A flock of our fellows are going to drive over by-and-by, and I'll be hanged if I don't make them buy every flower she's got, and camp down before her table afterwards," said Laurie, espousing her cause with warmth.

Thanks to the conspirators, the tables *were* turned that night. The March family turned out *en masse*, and Jo exerted herself to some purpose, for people not only came, but stayed, laughing at her nonsense, admiring Amy's taste, and apparently enjoying themselves very much. Laurie and his friends bought up the bouquets, encamped before the table, and made that corner the liveliest spot in the room. Amy was in her element now, and was as sprightly and gracious as possible—coming to the conclusion that virtue *was* its own reward after all.

Jo circulated about the hall, picking up various bits of gossip, which enlightened her upon the subject of the Chester change of base. As she passed the Art table, she glanced over it for her sister's things, but saw no signs of them.

" Tucked away out of sight, I dare say," thought Jo, who could forgive her own wrongs, but hotly resented any insult offered to her family.

" Good evening, Miss Jo ; how does Amy get on ? " asked May, with a conciliatory air—for she wanted to show that she also could be generous.

" She had sold everything she had that was worth selling, and now she is enjoying herself. The flower-table is always attractive, you know, ' especially to gentlemen.' "

Jo *couldn't* resist giving that little slap, but May took it so meekly she regretted it a minute after, and fell to praising the great vases, which still remained unsold.

" Is Amy's illumination anywhere about ? I took a fancy to buy that for father," said Jo.

" Everything of Amy's sold long ago ; I took care that the right people saw them, and they made a nice little sum of money for us," returned May, who had overcome sundry small temptations as well as Amy that day.

Much gratified, Jo rushed back to tell the good news ; and Amy looked both touched and surprised by the report of May's words and manner.

" Now, gentlemen, I want you to go and do your duty by the other tables as generously as you have by mine—especially the Art-table," she said, ordering out " Teddy's Own," as the girls called the college friends.

" ' Charge, Chester, charge ! ' is the motto for that table; but you'll get your money's worth of *art* in every sense of the word," said the irrepressible Jo, as the devoted phalanx prepared to take the field.

" Buy the vases," whispered Amy to Laurie, as a final heaping of coals of fire on her enemy's head.

" I leave Beth to your hands, then . . ."

[see page 57

Aunt Carrol was there, heard the story, looked pleased and said something to Mrs. March in a corner, which made the latter lady beam with satisfaction, though she did not betray the cause of her pleasure till several days later.

The fair was a pronounced success ; and when May bid Amy " good-night," she did not " gush," as usual, but gave her an affectionate kiss and a look which said " Forgive and forget." That satisfied Amy ; and when she got home she found the vases paraded on the parlour chimneypiece, with a great bouquet in each. " The reward of merit for a magnanimous March," as Laurie announced with a flourish.

" You've behaved sweetly, and I respect you with all my heart," said Jo, warmly, as they brushed their hair that night.

" Yes, we all do, and love her for being so ready to for- give. I don't believe I could have done it as kindly as you did," added Beth, from her pillow.

" Why, girls, you needn't praise me so ; I only did as I'd be done by. You laugh at me when I say I want to be a lady, but I mean a true gentlewoman in mind and manners, and I try to do it as far as I know how. I'm far from it now, but I do my best, and hope in time to be what mother is."

Amy spoke earnestly, and Jo said, with a cordial hug—
" Try away, deary, you'll get your reward some day, and no one will be more delighted than I shall."

A week later Amy did get her reward, and poor Jo found it hard to be delighted. A letter came from Aunt Carrol, and Mrs. March's face was illuminated to such a degree when she read it that Jo and Beth demanded what the glad tidings were.

" Aunt Carrol is going abroad next month, and wants——"
" Me to go with her ! " burst in Jo, flying out of her chair in an uncontrollable rapture.

No, dear, not you, it's Amy."

" Oh, mother ! she's too young ; it's my turn first It isn't fair, oh, it isn't fair ! " cried Jo, passionately.

" I'm afraid it is partly your own fault, dear. When aunt spoke to me the other day, she regretted your blunt manners and too independent spirit ; and here she writes as if quoting something you had said—' I planned at first to ask Jo ; but as " favours burden her," and she " hates

D

French " I think I won't venture to invite her. Amy is more docile, and will receive gratefully any help the trip may give her."

" Oh, my tongue, my abominable tongue ! why can't I learn to keep it quiet ? " groaned Jo, remembering words which had been her undoing. When she had heard the explanation of the quoted phrases, Mrs. March said, sorrowfully—

" I wish you could have gone, but there is no hope of it this time ; so try to bear it cheerfully, and don't sadden Amy's pleasure by reproaches or regrets."

" I'll try," said Jo, winking hard, as she knelt down to pick up the basket she had joyfully upset. " I'll take a leaf out of her book, and try not only to seem glad, but to be so, and not grudge her one minute of happiness ; but it won't be easy, for it is a dreadful disappointment."

" Jo, dear, I'm very selfish, but I couldn't spare you," whispered Beth, embracing her, basket and all, with such a clinging touch and loving face, that Jo felt comforted in spite of the sharp regret that made her want to box her own ears, and humbly beg Aunt Carrol to burden her with this favour, and see how gratefully she would bear it.

By the time Amy came in, Jo was able to take her part in the family jubilation. The young lady herself received the news in a solemn sort of rapture, and began to sort her colours and pack her pencils, leaving such trifles as clothes, money, and passports to those less absorbed in art than herself.

" Girls," she said impressively, as she scraped her best palette. " It will decide my career ; for if I have any genius, I shall find it out in Rome."

" Suppose you haven't ? " said Jo, sewing away, with red eyes, at the new collars which were to be handed over to Amy.

" Then I shall come home and teach drawing for my living."

" No you won't ; you'll marry some rich man, and sit in the lap of luxury all your days," said Jo.

" Your predictions sometimes come to pass, but I don't believe that one will. I'm sure I wish it would, for if I can't be an artist myself, I should like to be able to help those who are," said Amy, adding thoughtfully, " Would you like to go ? "

·" Rather ! "

" Well, in a year or two I'll send for you, and we'll carry out all the plans we've made so many times."

" Thank you ; I'll remind you of your promise when that joyful day comes, if it ever does," returned Jo, accepting the offer as gratefully as she could.

There was not much time for preparation, and the house was in a ferment till Amy was off. Jo bore up very well till the last flutter of blue ribbon vanished, when she retired to her refuge the garret, and cried till she couldn't cry any more. Amy likewise bore up stoutly till the steamer sailed ; then, just as the gangway was about to be withdrawn, it suddenly came over her that a whole ocean was soon to roll between her and those who loved her best, and she clung to Laurie, saying with a sob—

" Oh, take care of them for me ; and if anything should happen—— "

" I will, dear, I will ; and if anything happens, I'll come and comfort you," whispered Laurie, little dreaming how soon he would be called upon to keep his word.

CHAPTER VIII

OUR FOREIGN CORRESPONDENT

" LONDON.

" DEAREST PEOPLE :

" Here I sit at a front window of the Bath Hotel, Piccadilly. Oh, I can't begin to tell you how I enjoy it all, so I'll only give you bits out of my notebook, for I've done nothing but sketch and scribble since I started.

" I sent a line from Halifax when I felt pretty miserable, but after that I got on delightfully, seldom ill, on deck all day, with plenty of pleasant people to amuse me.

" Aunt and Flo were poorly all the way, and liked to be let alone, so when I had done what I could for them, I went and enjoyed myself. Such walks on deck, such sunsets, such splendid air and waves !

" At Queenstown one of my new acquaintances left us—
Mr. Lennox. We only stopped at Liverpool a few hours
but that absurd Lennox got his friend Ward, who came on
with us, to order a bouquet for me, and the first thing I saw
in my room, was a lovely one, with ' Robert Lennox's compliments ' on the card. Wasn't that fun, girls ? I like
travelling.

" The trip was like riding through a long picture-gallery,
full of lovely landscapes. The farmhouses were my delight ;
with thatched roofs, ivy up to the eaves, latticed windows,
and stout women with rosy children at the doors. I was in
a rapture all the way. So was Flo ; and we kept bouncing
from one side to the other, trying to see everything while
we were whisking along at the rate of sixty miles an hour.
Aunt went to sleep, but uncle read his guide-book, and
wouldn't be astonished at anything. This is the way we
went on : Amy flying up—Oh, that must be Kenilworth,
that grey place among the trees ! ' Flo darting to my
window—' How sweet ; we must go there sometime, won't
we, pa ? Uncle calmly—' No, my dear, not unless you
want beer ; that's a brewery.'

" After that Flo settles down to enjoy *The Flirtations of
Capt. Cavendish*, and I have the scenery all to myself.

" Of course it rained when we got to London, and there
was nothing to be seen but fog and umbrellas. Aunt Mary
got me some new things, for I came off in such a hurry I
wasn't half ready. Shopping in Regent street is perfectly
splendid ; things seem so cheap—nice ribbons only sixpence a yard. I laid in a stock, but shall get my
gloves in Paris. Doesn't that sound sort of elegant and
rich ?

" To-day was fair, and we went to Hyde Park, close by.
Such sights as I saw, my dear ! It was as good as Punch,
for there were fat dowagers, rolling about in their red and
yellow coaches, with gorgeous Jeameses in silk stockings
and velvet coats, up behind, and powdered coachmen in
front.

" Rotten Row means ' *Route de Roi*,' or the king's way ;
but now it's more like a riding-school than anything else.
Everyone rides—old men, stout ladies, little children, and
the young folks do a deal of flirting here ; I saw a pair
exchange rose-buds, for it's the thing to wear one in the
button-hole, and I thought it rather a nice little idea.

' In the p.m. to Westminster Abbey ; but don't expect
me to describe it, that's impossible—so I'll only say it was
sublime ! "

" *Midnight*.

" It's very late, but I can't let my letter go in the morning
without telling you what happened last evening. Who do
you think came in, as we were at tea ? Laurie's English
friends, Fred and Frank Vaughn ! I was so surprised
for I shouldn't have known them, but for the cards. They
went to the theatre with us, and we did have *such* a good
time, for Frank devoted himself to Flo, and Fred and I
talked over the past, present and future fun as if we had
kno n each other all our days.

" Aunt is tapping on the wall for the third time, so I
must stop. I long to see you all, and in spite of my nonsense am, as ever, your loving

" Amy."

" Paris.

" Dear Girls—
" In my last I told you about our London visit,—how
kind the Vaughns were, and what pleasant parties they
made for us. I enjoyed the trips to Hampton Court and
the Kensington Museum, more than anything else,—for at
Hampton I saw Raphael's Cartoons, and, at the Museum,
rooms full of pictures by Turner, Lawrence, Reynolds,
Hogarth, and the other great creatures. The Vaughns
hope to meet us in Rome next winter, and I shall be
dreadfully disappointed if they don't, for Grace and I are
great friends, and the boys very nice fellows,—especially
Fred.

" Well, we were hardly settled here when he turned up
again, saying he had come for a holiday, and was going
to Switzerland. Aunt looked sober at first, but he was so
cool about it she couldn't say a word ; and now we get on
nicely, and are very glad he came, for he speaks French
like a native, and I don't know what we should do without
him.

" Such delightful times as we are having ! sight-seeing
from morning till night ! stopping for nice lunches in the
gay *cafés*, and meeting with all sorts of droll adventures.

" The Palais Royale is a heavenly place, and the Bois

and the Champs Elysées are *très magnifique*. I've seen the imperial family several times,—the Emperor an ugly, hard-looking man, the Empress pale and pretty, but dressed in horrid taste, *I* thought,—purple dress, green hat, and yellow gloves. We often walk in the Tuileries gardens, for they are lovely, though the antique Luxembourg gardens suit me better. Our rooms are on the Rue de Rivoli, and sitting on the balcony, we look up and down the long, brilliant street. It is so pleasant that we spend our evenings talking there,—when too tired with our day's work to go out.

" Next week we are off to Germany and Switzerland ; and, as we shall travel fast, I shall only be able to give you hasty letters. I keep my diary, and try to ' remember correctly and describe clearly all that I see and admire,' as father advised. It is good practice for me, and, with my sketch-book, will give you a better idea of my tour than these scribbles.

" Adieu ; I embrace you tenderly.

" VOTRE AMIE."

" HEIDELBERG.

" MY DEAR MAMMA—

" Having a quiet hour before we leave for Berne, I'll try to tell you what has happened, for some of it is very important, as you will see.

" The sail up the Rhine was perfect, and I just sat and enjoyed it with all my might. Get father's old guide-books, and read about it ; I haven't words beautiful enough to describe it. At Coblentz we had a lovely time, for some students from Bonn, with whom Fred got acquainted on the boat, gave us a serenade. It was a moonlight night, and, about one o'clock, Flo and I were waked by the most delicious music under our windows. It was the most romantic thing I ever saw ; the river, the bridge of boats, the great fortress opposite, moonlight everywhere, and music fit to melt a heart of stone.

" When they were done we threw down some flowers, and saw them scramble for them, kiss their hands to the invisible ladies and go laughing away,—to smoke, and drink beer, I suppose. Next morning Fred showed me one of the crumpled flowers in his vest pocket, and looked very sentimental. I laughed at him, and said I didn't throw it, but Flo,—which seemed to disgust him, for he tossed it out of the window, and turned sensible again.

"Now comes the serious part,—for it happened here, and Fred is just gone. He has been so kind and jolly that we all got quite fond of him ; I never thought of anything but a travelling friendship, till the serenade night. Since then I've begun to feel that the moonlight walks and daily adventures were something more to him than fun. I haven't flirted, mother, truly,—but remembered what you said to me, and have done my very best. Now I know mother will shake her head, and the girls say, 'Oh, the mercenary little wretch ! ' but I've made up my mind, and, if Fred asks me, I shall accept him, though I'm not madly in love. I like him, and we get on comfortably together. He is handsome, young, clever enough, and very rich,— ever so much richer than the Laurences, I don't think his family would object, and I should be very happy, for they are all kind, well-bred, generous people, and they like me. I may be mercenary, but I hate poverty, and don't mean to bear it a minute longer than I can help. One of us *must* marry well ; Meg didn't, Jo won't, Beth can't, yet,—so I shall, and make everything cosy all round. I've been turning the matter over in my mind the last week—for it was impossible to help seeing that Fred liked me.

"Well, last evening we went up to the castle about sunset,—at least all of us but Fred, who was to meet us there after going to the Poste Restante for letters. We had a charming time poking about the ruins, the vaults where the monster tun is, and the beautiful gardens made by the Elector, long ago, for his English wife. I felt as if I'd got into a romance, sitting there watching the Neckar rolling through the valley, listening to the music of the Austrian band below, and waiting for my lover,—like a real story-book girl.

"By-and-by I heard Fred's voice, and then he came hurrying through the great arch to find me. He said he'd just got a letter begging him to come home, for Frank was very ill ; so he was going at once, in the night train, and only had time to say 'good-bye.' I was very sorry for him, and he said, as he shook hands,—'I shall soon come back—you won't forget me, Amy ? '

"I didn't promise, but I looked at him, and he seemed

satisfied—and there was no time for anything but messages and good-byes, for he was off in an hour, and we all miss him very much. We shall soon meet in Rome ; and then, if I don't change my mind, I'll say ' Yes, thank you,' when he says ' Will you, please ? '

" Of course this is all *very private*, but I wished you to know what was going on. Send me as much advice as you like ; I'll use it if I can. I wish I could see you for a good talk, Marmee. Love and trust me.

" Ever your
" AMY."

CHAPTER IX

TENDER TROUBLES

" Jo, I'm anxious about Beth."

" Why, mother, she has seemed unusually well since the babies came."

" It's not her health that troubles me now ; it's her spirits. I'm sure there is something on her mind, and I want you to discover what it is."

" What makes you think so, mother ? "

" She sits alone a good deal, and doesn't talk to her father as much as she used. I found her crying the other day. This isn't like Beth, and it worries me."

" Have you asked her about it ? "

" I have tried once or twice, but she looked so distressed, that I stopped. After sewing thoughtfully for a minute, Jo said,—

" I think she is growing up, and begins to dream dreams, without knowing why, or being able to explain them. Why, mother, Beth's eighteen ; but we treat her like a child, forgetting she's a woman."

" So she is ; dear, how fast you do grow up," returned her mother, with a sigh and a smile.

" Can't be helped, Marmee ; so you must let your birds

hop out of the nest, one by one. I promise never to hop very far, if that is any comfort to you."

" It is a great comfort, Jo ; I always feel strong when you are at home, now Meg is gone."

" Why, you know I don't mind hard jobs and feel in my element when all the carpets are to be taken up, or half the family fall sick at once. Amy is distinguishing herself abroad ; but if anything is amiss at home, I'm your man."

" I leave Beth to your hands then, for she will open her heart to her Jo sooner than to anyone else. If she only would get strong and cheerful again, I shouldn't have a wish in the world."

" I've got heaps, but I'll settle Bethy's troubles, and then I'll tell you mine. They are not very wearying, so they'll keep ; " and Jo stitched away with a wise nod, which set her mother's heart at rest about her, for the present at least.

While apparently absorbed in her own affairs, Jo watched Beth ; and after many conjectures, finally settled upon one which seemed to explain the change in her. She was affecting to write busily one Saturday afternoon, when she and Beth were alone together ; yet, as she scribbled, she kept her eye on her sister, who seemed unusually quiet. Sitting at the window, Beth leaned her head upon her hand, in a dejected attitude, until suddenly someone passed below, and a voice called out,—

" All serene ! Coming in to-night."

Beth started, leaned forward smiled and watched the passer-by till his quick tramp died away, then said softly,—

" How strong, and well, and happy that dear boy looks."

" Hum ! " said Jo, still intent upon her sister's face ; for the bright colour faded as quickly as it came, and presently a tear lay shining on the window-ledge. Beth whisked it off, and glanced apprehensively at Jo ; but she was scratching away at a tremendous rate, apparently engrossed in " Olympia's Oath." The instant Beth turned, Jo began her watch again, saw Beth's hand go quietly to her eyes more than once, and, in her half-averted face, read a tender sorrow that made her own eyes fill. Fearing to betray herself, she slipped away, murmuring something about needing more paper.

"Mercy on me, Beth loves Laurie!" she said, sitting down in her own room, pale with the shock of the discovery which she believed she had just made. "I never dreamt of such a thing! What *will* mother say? I wonder if he—" there Jo stopped, and turned scarlet with a sudden thought. "If he shouldn't love back again, how dreadful it would be. He must; I'll make him! Oh dear, we *are* growing up with a vengeance. Here's Meg married, Amy flourishing away at Paris, and Beth in love. I'm the only one that has sense enough to keep out of mischief."

Though Laurie flirted with Amy, and joked with Jo, his manner to Beth had always been peculiarly kind and gentle, but so was everybody's; therefore, no one thought of imagining that he cared more for her than for the others. Indeed, a general impression had prevailed in the family, of late, that "our boy" was getting fonder than ever of Jo, who, however, wouldn't hear a word upon the subject, and scolded violently if any one dared to suggest it.

When Laurie first went to college, he fell in love about once a month; but these small flames were as brief as ardent, and much amused Jo, who took great interest in the alternations of hope, despair, and resignation, which were confided to her in their weekly conferences. But there came a time when Laurie ceased to worship at many shrines, hinted darkly at one all-absorbing passion, and indulged occasionally in Byronic fits of gloom.

Things were in this state when the grand discovery was made, and Jo watched Laurie that night as she had never done before. If she had not got the new idea into her head, she would have seen nothing unusual in the fact, that Beth was very quiet, and Laurie very kind to her. But having given the rein to her lively fancy, it galloped away with her at a great pace; and common sense, being rather weakened by a long course of romance writing, did not come to the rescue.

"Who knows! stranger things have happened," thought Jo, as she fussed about the room. "She will make quite an angel of him, and he will make life delightfully easy and pleasant for the dear, if they only love each other."

Now the old sofa was Jo's favourite lounging place. Among the many pillows that adorned the venerable couch was one, hard, round, covered with prickly horse-hair, and furnished with a knobby button at each end. This was

her especial property, being used as a weapon of defence,
a barricade, or a stern preventive of too much slumber.

Laurie knew this pillow well, having been unmercifully
pummelled with it in former days, when romping was
allowed, and now frequently debarred by it from taking
the seat he most coveted, next to Jo in the sofa corner.
That evening Jo forgot to barricade her corner, and had
not been in her seat five minutes, before a massive form
appeared beside her, and with both arms spread over the
sofa back, both long legs stretched out before him, Laurie
exclaimed with a sigh of satisfaction,—

" Now *this* is filling at the price ! "

" No slang," snapped Jo, slamming down the pillow.
But it was too late—there was no room for it ; and coasting
on to the floor, it disappeared in a most mysterious manner.

" Come, Jo, don't be thorny. After studying himself to
a skeleton all the week, a fellow deserves petting."

" Beth will pet you, I'm busy."

" No, she's not to be bothered with me. Do you hate
your boy, and want to fire pillows at him ? "

Anything more wheedlesome than that touching appeal
was seldom seen, but Jo quenched " her boy " by turning
on him with the stern query,—

" How many bouquets have you sent Miss Randal this
week ? "

" Not one, upon my word ! She's engaged. Now then ! "

" I'm glad of it ; that's one of your foolish extrava-
gances, sending flowers and things to girls for whom you
don't care two pins," continued Jo, reprovingly.

" Sensible girls, for whom I do care whole papers of pins,
won't let me send them ' flowers and things,' so what can
I do ? my feelings must have a *went*."

" Mother doesn't approve of flirting, even in fun ; and
you do flirt desperately, Teddy."

" Much you know about it, ma'am ! " said Laurie, in a
superior tone. " Bless your innocent soul, if you could be
in my place for a month you'd see things that would
astonish you a trifle."

Jo knew that " young Laurence " was regarded as a
most eligible *parti* by worldly mammas, was much smiled
upon by their daughters, and flattered enough by ladies of
all ages to make a coxcomb of him ; so she watched him
rather jealously, fearing he would be spoilt, and rejoiced

more than she confessed to find that he still believed in
modest girls.   Returning suddenly to her admonitory tone,
she said, dropping her voice, " If you must have a ' went,'
Teddy, go and devote yourself to one of the ' pretty modest
girls,' whom you respect ; don't waste your time with the
silly ones."

" You really advise it ? " and Laurie looked at her with
an odd mixture of anxiety and merriment in his face.

" Yes, I do ; but you'd better wait till you are through
college, on the whole, and be fitting yourself for the place
meantime.   You're not half good enough for—well, who-
ever the modest girl may be ; " and Jo looked a little queer
likewise, for a name had almost escaped her.

" That I'm not ! " acquiesced Laurie, with an expression
of humility quite new to him, as he dropped his eyes, and
absently wound Jo's apron tassel round his finger.

" Go and sing to me.   I'm dying for some music,"
demanded Jo, diving for the pillow.

He fled at once, and the minute it was well " Up with
the bonnets of bonnie Dundee," she slipped away, to
return no more till the young gentleman had departed in
high dudgeon.

Jo lay long awake that night, and was just dropping off
when the sound of a stifled sob made her fly to Beth's
bedside, with the anxious inquiry, " What is it, dear ? "

" I thought you were asleep," sobbed Beth.

" Is it the old pain, my precious ? "

" No ; it's a new one ; but I can bear it," and Beth
tried to check her tears.

" Tell me all about it, and let me cure it as I often did
the other."

" You can't ; there is no cure."   There Beth's voice gave
way, and she cried so despairingly that Jo was frightened.

" Where is it ?   Shall I call mother ? "

Beth did not answer the first question ; but held Jo fast,
whispering eagerly,—

" No, no, don't tell her ! I shall be better soon.   Lie
down here and I'll be quiet, and go to sleep, indeed I will."

Jo obeyed ; but as her hand went softly to and fro
across Beth's hot forehead and wet eyelids, her heart was
very full, and she longed to speak.   But she only said, in
her tenderest tone, " Does anything trouble you, deary ? "

" Yes, Jo ! " after a long pause.

" Wouldn't it comfort you to tell me what it is ? "

" Not now, not yet."

" Then I won't ask ; but remember, Bethy, that mother and Jo are always glad to hear and help you, if they can."

" I know it. I'll tell you by-and-by."

" Is the pain better now ? "

" Oh, yes, much better ; you are so comfortable, Jo ! "

" Go to sleep, dear ; I'll stay with you."

So cheek to cheek they fell asleep, and on the morrow Jo made up her mind, and, after pondering over a project, she confided it to her mother.

" You asked me the other day what my wishes were. I'll tell you one of them, Marmee," she began, as they sat alone together. " I want to go away this winter for a change."

" Why, Jo ? " and her mother looked up quickly, as if the words suggested a double meaning.

With her eyes on her work, Jo answered soberly, " I want something new ; I feel restless and anxious to be seeing, doing, and learning more than I am. I'd like to hop a little way and try my wings."

" Where will you hop ? "

" To New York. You know Mrs. Kirke wrote to you for some respectable young person to teach her children, and sew. I think I should suit if I tried."

" My dear, go out to service in that great boarding-house ! " and Mrs. March looked surprised, but not displeased.

" It's not exactly going out to service ; for Mrs. Kirke is your friend, and would make things pleasant for me I know. It's honest work, and I'm not ashamed of it."

" Nor I ; but your writing ? "

" All the better for the change. I shall see and hear new things, get new ideas, and bring home quantities of material for my rubbish."

" I have no doubt of it ; but are these your only reasons ? "

" No, mother."

" May I know the others ? "

Jo looked up and Jo looked down, then said slowly, " It may be vain and wrong to say it, but—I'm afraid—Laurie is getting too fond of me."

" Then you don't care for him in the way he begins to
care for you ? " Mrs. March asked anxiously.

" Mercy, no ! I love the dear boy, and am immensely
proud of him ; but anything more is out of the question."

" I'm glad of that, Jo, because I don't think you're suited
to one another.   As friends, you are very happy, and your
frequent quarrels soon blow over ; but I fear you would
both rebel if you were mated for life.   You are too much
alike, and too fond of freedom, to get on happily together,
in a relation which needs infinite patience, as well as
love."

" That's just the feeling I had, though I couldn't express
it.   I'm glad you think he is only beginning to care for me.
I think I had better go away before it comes to anything."

" I agree with you, and if it can be managed you shall go."
Jo looked relieved, and, after a pause, said, smiling,—

" How Mrs. Moffat would wonder at your want of
management, if she knew.

" Ah, Jo, mothers may differ in their management, but
the hope is the same in all—the desire to see their children
happy.   Amy is my chief care now, but her good sense
will help her.   For Beth, I indulge no hopes except that
she may be well.   By the way, she seems brighter this last
day or two.   Have you spoken to her ? "

" Yes ;   she owned she had a trouble, and promised to
tell me by-and-by, but I think I know it ; " and Jo told
her little story.

Mrs. March shook her head, and did not take so romantic
a view of the case, but looked grave, and repeated her
opinion that, for Laurie's sake, Jo should go away for a
time.

" Let us say nothing about it to him till the plan is
settled ; then I'll run away before he can collect his wits
and be tragical.   Beth can pet and comfort him after
I'm gone, and so cure him of this romantic notion."

The plan was talked over in a family council, and agreed
upon ; for Mrs. Kirke gladly accepted Jo, and promised
to make a pleasant home for her.   The teaching would
render her independent ; and such leisure as she got might
be made profitable by writing, while the new scenes and
society would be both useful and agreeable.   When all
was settled, with fear and trembling she told Laurie ; but

to her surprise, he took it very quietly ; only when they said " Good-bye," he whispered significantly, " It won't do a bit of good, Jo. My eye is on you ; so mind what you do, or I'll come and bring you home."

CHAPTER X

JO'S JOURNAL

" NEW YORK, NOV.

" DEAR MARMEE AND BETH—

" I'm going to write you a regular volume, for I've got lots to tell, though I'm not a fine young lady travelling on the Continent.

" Mrs. Kirke welcomed me so kindly I felt at home at once, even in that big house full of strangers. She gave me a funny little sky-parlour—all she had ; but there is a stove in it, and a nice table in a sunny window, so I can sit here and write whenever I like. The nursery, where I am to teach and sew, is a pleasant room next Mrs. Kirke's private parlour, and the two little girls are pretty children —and I've no doubt I shall make a model governess.

" ' Now my dear, make yourself at home,' said Mrs. K in her motherly way. My rooms are always open to you, and your own shall be as comfortable as I can make it. There are some pleasant people in the house, if you feel sociable, and your evenings are always free. Come to me if anything goes wrong, and be as happy as you can.' And off she bustled, leaving me to settle myself in my new nest.

" As I went downstairs, soon after, I saw something I liked. As I stood waiting at the head of the third flight for a little servant girl to lumber up, I saw a man come along behind her, take the heavy hod of coal out of her hand, carry it all the way up, and walk away, saying, with a kind nod and a foreign accent,—

" ' It goes better so. The little back is too young to haf such heaviness.'

"Wasn't it good of him ? I like such things ; for, as
father says, trifles show character. When I mentioned it
to Mrs. K., that evening, she laughed, and said,—

"'That must have been Professor Bhaer ; he's always
doing things of that sort.'

"Mrs. K. told me he was from Berlin, and gives lessons
to support himself and two little orphan nephews, Franz
and Emil, whom he is educating here. Mrs. K. lends him
her parlour for some of his scholars. There is a glass door
between it and the nursery, and I mean to peep at him,
and then I'll tell you how he looks.

"After tea I attacked the big work-basket, and had a
quiet evening chatting with my new friend. I shall keep
a journal letter, and send it once a week ; so good-night
and more to-morrow."

                                        "*Tuesday Eve.*

"Had a lively time in my seminary, this morning, and
at one time I really thought I should shake the children
all round. Some good angel inspired me to try gymnastics,
and I kept it up till they were glad to sit down and keep
still. After luncheon, the girl took them out for a walk,
and I went to my needle-work. I was thanking my stars
that I'd learned to make nice button-holes, when the
parlour door opened and shut, and some one began to
hum,—

              'Kennst du das land '

like a big bumble-bee. It was dreadfully improper, I know,
but I couldn't resist the temptation ; and lifting one end
of the curtain before the glass door, I peeped in. Professor
Bhaer was there ; and while he arranged his books, I took
a good look at him. A regular German—rather stout, with
brown hair tumbled all over his head, the kindest eyes I
ever saw, and a splendid big voice that does one's ears
good, after our American gabble. I liked him, for he had
a fine head ; his linen was nice, and he looked like a gentleman, though two buttons were off his coat, and there was
a patch on one shoe. He went to the window to turn the
hyacinth bulbs towards the sun, and stroke the cat, who
received him like an old friend. Then he smiled ; and
when a tap came at the door, called out in a loud, brisk
tone,—

" ' Herein ! '

" I was just going to run when I caught sight of a child carrying a big book, and stopped to see what was going on.

" ' Me wants my Bhaer,' said the mite, slamming down her book, and running to meet him.

" ' Thou shalt haf thy Bhaer ; come, then, and take a goot hug from him, my Tina,' said the Professor, catching her up, with a laugh, and holding her so high over his head that she had to stoop her little face to kiss him.

" ' Now me mus tuddy my lessin,' went on the funny little thing ; so he put her up at the table, opened the great dictionary she had brought, and gave her a paper and pencil, and she scribbled away, passing her fat little finger down the page, as if finding a word, so soberly, that I nearly betrayed myself by a laugh, while Mr. Bhaer stood stroking her hair, with a fatherly look, till the clock struck two, when he put his books in his pocket, as if ready for another lesson, and, taking little Tina in his arms, he carried her away.

" *Thursday.*

" Yesterday was a quiet day, spent in teaching, sewing, and writing in my little room,—which is very cosy, with a light and fire. I picked up a few bits of news and was introduced to the Professor. It seems that Tina is the child of the Frenchwoman who does the fine ironing in the laundry here. The little thing has lost her heart to Mr. Bhaer, and follows him about the house like a dog whenever he is at home, which delights him,—as he is very fond of children, though a ' bacheldore.' Kitty and Minnie Kirke likewise regard him with affection, and tell all sorts of stories about the plays he invents, the presents he brings, and the splendid tales he tells.

" I was in our parlour last evening, when Mr. Bhaer came in with some newspapers for Mrs. Kirke. She wasn't there, but Minnie, who is a little old woman, introduced me very prettily : ' This is mamma's friend, Miss March.'

" ' Yes ; and she's jolly, and we like her lots,' added Kitty, who is an ' *enfant terrible.*'

" We both bowed, and then we laughed, for the prim introduction and the blunt addition were rather a comical contrast.

" ' Ah, yes ; I hear these naughty ones go to vex you,

E

Mees Marsch.   If so again, call at me and I come,' he said,
with a threatening frown that delighted the little wretches.

"They played tag, and soldiers, danced and sung, and
when it began to grow dark they all piled on to the sofa
about the professor, while he told charming fairy stories of
the storks on the chimney-tops, and the little 'Kobolds,'
who ride the snowflakes as they fall.   I wish Americans
were as simple and natural as Germans, don't you ?

"I'm so fond of writing, I should go spinning on for ever
if motives of economy didn't stop me ; for though I've
used thin paper and written fine, I tremble to think of the
stamps this long letter will need.   Pray forward Amy's as
soon as you can spare them.   My small news will sound
very flat after her splendours, but you will like them, I
know.   Is Teddy studying so hard that he can't find time
to write to his friends ? Take good care of him for me, Beth,
and tell me about the babies, and give heaps of love to
everyone.

" From your faithful

" Jo.

"P.S.—On reading over my letter, it strikes me as
rather Bhaery ; but I'm always interested in odd people,
and I really had nothing else to write about.   Bless you."

" Dec.

"MY PRECIOUS BETSEY—

"As this is to be a scribble-scrabble letter, I direct it
to you, for it may amuse you, and give you some ideas of
my goings on.   After what Amy would call Herculaneum
efforts, in the way of mental and moral agriculture, my
young ideas begin to shoot, and my little twigs to bend, as
I could wish.   Franz and Emil are jolly little lads, quite
after my own heart, for the mixture of German and
American spirit in them produces a constant state of effer-
vescence.   Saturday afternoons are riotous times, whether
spent in the house or out ; for on pleasant days they all go
to walk, like a seminary, with the Professor and myself to
keep order ; and then such fun !

"We are very good friends now, and I've begun to take
lessons.   Mrs. Kirke called to me, one day, as I passed
Mr. Bhaer's room, where she was rummaging.

"'Did you ever see such a den, my dear ?   Just come
and help me to put these books to rights, for I've turned

everything upside down, trying to discover what he has done with the six new handkerchiefs I gave him not long ago.'

" After a grand rummage, three of the missing articles were found,—one over the bird-cage, one covered with ink, and a third burnt brown, having been used as a holder.

" ' Such a man ! " laughed good-natured Mrs. K., as she put the relics in the rag-bag. " I agreed to do his washing and mending, but he forgets to give out his things, and comes to a sad pass sometimes.'

" ' Let me mend them,' said I ; ' I don't mind it, and he needn't know. I'd like to,—he's so kind to me about bringing my letters, and lending books.'

" So I have got his things in order, and knit heels into two pairs of his socks,—for they were boggled out of shape with his queer darns. Nothing was said, and I hoped he wouldn't find it out, but one day last week he caught me at it. I had been sitting near the parlour door, finishing off the last sock, and rocking to and fro in a most absurd way, when a little crow made me look up, and there was Mr. Bhaer looking and laughing quietly.

" ' So,' he said, as I stopped and stared like a goose, ' you peep at me, I peep at you, and that is not bad ; but see, I am not pleasanting when I say, haf you a wish for German ? '

" ' Yes ; but you are too busy ; I am too stupid to learn,' I blundered out, as red as a beet.

" ' Prut ! we will make the time, and we fail not to find the sense. At efening I shall gif a little lesson with much gladness ; for, look you, Mees Marsch, I haf this debt to pay,' and he pointed to my work. ' Yes ! they say to one another, these so kind ladies, " he is a stupid old fellow ; he will see not what we do ; he will never opserve that his sock-heels go not in holes any more ; he will think his buttons grow out new when they fall, and believe that strings make theirselves." Ah ! but I haf an eye, and I see much. I haf a heart, and I feel the thanks for this. Come,—a little lesson then and now, or—no more good fairy works for me and mine.'

" Of course I couldn't say anything after that, and as it really is a splendid opportunity, I made the bargain, and we began. The Professor was very patient with me, but it must have been torment to him, and now and then he'd look at me with such an expression of mild despair, that

it was a toss up with me whether to laugh or cry. I tried
both ways ; and when it grew to a sniff of utter mortification
and woe, he just threw the grammar on to the floor, and
marched out of the room. I felt myself disgraced and
deserted for ever, but didn't blame him a particle, and was
scrambling my papers together, meaning to rush upstairs
when in he came, as brisk and beaming as if I'd covered
my name with glory :—

" ' Now we shall try a new way. You and I will read
these pleasant little Märchen together, and dig no more in
that dry book, that goes in the corner for making us
trouble.'

" He spoke so kindly, and opened Hans Andersen's fairy
tales so invitingly before me, that I was more ashamed
than ever, and went at my lesson in a neck-or-nothing style
that seemed to amuse him immensely. When I finished
reading my first page, and stopped for breath, he clapped
his hands and cried out, in his hearty way, ' Das ist gute !
Now we go well ! My turn. I do him in German ; gif
me your ear.' And away he went, rumbling out the words
with his strong voice, and a relish which was good to see as
well as hear.

" After that we got on better, and now I read my lessons
pretty well ; for this way of studying suits me, and I can
see that the grammar gets tucked into the tales and poetry,
as one gives pills in jelly.

" I'm glad Laurie seems so happy and busy. You see
Beth manages him better than I did. I'm afraid I couldn't
like him without a spice of human naughtiness. Read him
bits of my letters. I haven't time to write much, and that
will do just as well. Thank Heaven Beth continues so
comfortable."

                                                    " *Jan.*
" A happy New-Year to you all, my dearest family,
which of course includes Mr. L. and a young man by the
name of Teddy. I can't tell you how much I enjoyed
your Christmas bundle, for I didn't get it till night, and
had given up hoping. It was so *homey* and refreshing, that
I sat down on the floor, and read, and looked, and ate, and
laughed and cried, in my usual absurd way. The things
were just what I wanted, and all the better for being made
instead of bought. Thank you all, heaps and heaps !

"Mr. Bhaer gave me a fine Shakespeare. It is one he values much, and I've often admired it, set up in the place of honour, with his German Bible, Plato, Homer, and Milton ; so you may imagine how I felt when he brought it down, without its cover, and showed me my name in it, 'from my friend Friedrich Bhaer.'

"'You say often you wish a library ; here I gif you one ; for between these two lids' (he meant covers) 'is many books in one. Read him well, and he will help you much ; for the study of character in this book will help you to read it in the world, and paint it with your pen.'

"I thanked him as well as I could, and talk now about 'my library,' as if I had a hundred books.

"Not having much money, or knowing what he'd like, I got several little things, and put them about the room, where he would find them unexpectedly. Poor as he is, he didn't forget a servant or a child in the house ; and not a soul here, from the French laundry-woman to Miss Norton, forgot him. I was so glad of that.

"They got up a masquerade and had a gay time, New-Year's Eve. I didn't mean to go down, having no dress ; but at the last minute, Mrs. Kirke remembered some old brocades, and Miss Norton lent me lace and feathers ; so I rigged up as Mrs. Malaprop, and sailed in with a mask on.

"I had a very happy New-Year, after all ; for I'm cheerful all the time now, work with a will, and take more interest in other people than I used to, which is satisfactory. Bless you all.

"Ever your loving
"Jo."

CHAPTER XI

A FRIEND

THOUGH very happy in the social atmosphere about her, and very busy with the daily work that earned her bread, and made it sweeter for the effort, Jo still found time for

literary labours. The purpose which now took possession
of her was a natural one to a poor and ambitious girl ; but
the means she took to gain her end were not the best.
She saw that money conferred power; money and power,
therefore, she resolved to have ; not to be used for herself
alone, but for those whom she loved more than self. She
told no one, but concocted a " thrilling tale," and boldly
carried it herself to Mr. Dashwood, editor of the *Weekly
Volcano*. She had never read *Sartor Resartus*, but she had
a womanly instinct that clothes possess an influence more
powerful over many than the worth of character or the
magic of manners. So she dressed herself in her best, and
bravely climbed two pairs of dark and dirty stairs to find
herself in the presence of three gentlemen sitting with their
heels rather higher than their hats, which articles of dress
none of them took the trouble to remove on her appearance.
Somewhat daunted by this reception, Jo hesitated on the
threshold, murmuring in much embarrassment,—

" Excuse me ; I wished to see Mr. Dashwood."

Down went the highest pair of heels, up rose the smokiest
gentleman, and, carefully cherishing his cigar between his
fingers, he advanced with a nod. Feeling that she must
get through with the matter somehow, Jo produced her
manuscript, and blundered out fragments of the little
speech carefully prepared for the occasion.

" A friend of mine desired me to offer—a story—would
like your opinion—be glad to write more if this suits."

While she blushed and blundered, Mr. Dashwood had
taken the manuscript, and was turning over the leaves,
casting critical glances up and down the neat pages.

" Not a first attempt, I take it ? " observing that the
pages were covered only on one side, and *not* tied up with
a ribbon—sure sign of a novice.

" No, sir ; she has had some experience, and got a prize
for a tale in the *Blarneystone Banner*."

" Oh, did she ? " and Mr. Dashwood gave Jo a quick
look, which seemed to take note of everything she had
on. " Well, you can leave it, if you like ; I'll run my eye
over it, and give you an answer next week."

Now Jo did *not* like to leave it, for Mr. Dashwood didn't
suit her at all ; but, under the circumstances there was
nothing for her to do but bow and walk away, looking
particularly tall and dignified, as she was apt to do, when

nettled or abashed. Just then she was both ; for it was
perfectly evident from the knowing glances exchanged
among the gentlemen, that her little fiction of " my
friend " was considered a good joke ; and a laugh produced
by some inaudible remark of the editor, as he closed the
door completed her discomfiture. Half resolving never to
return, she went home, and worked off her irritation by
stitching pinafores vigorously ; and in an hour or two was
cool enough to laugh over the scene, and long for next
week.

When she went again, Mr. Dashwood was alone, whereat
she rejoiced. Mr. Dashwood was much wider awake than
before, so the second interview was much more comfortable
than the first.

" We'll take this, if you don't object to a few alterations.
It's too long, but omitting the passages I've marked will
make it the right length," he said, in a businesslike tone.

Jo hardly knew her own MS. again, so crumpled and
under-scored were its pages and paragraphs ; she looked
at the marked passages, and was surprised to find that all
the moral reflections had been struck out.

" But I thought every story should have a moral."

Mr. Dashwood's editorial gravity relaxed into a smile,
for Jo had forgotten her " friend," and spoken as only an
author could.

" People want to be amused, not preached at, you
know. We give from twenty-five to thirty for things of
this sort. Pay when it comes out," returned Mr. Dashwood.

" Very well ; you can have it," said Jo, handing back the
story. " Shall I tell my friend you will take another if
she has one better than this ? " she added, unconscious of
her little slip of the tongue, and emboldened by her success.

" Well, we'll look at it ; can't promise to take it ; tell
her to make it short and spicy, and never mind the moral.
What name would your friend like to put to it ? " in a
careless tone.

" None at all, if you please ; she doesn't wish her name
to appear, and has no *nom de plume*," said Jo, blushing.

" Just as she likes, of course. The tale will be out next
week ; will you call for the money, or shall I send it ? "
asked Mr. Dashwood, who felt a natural desire to know
who his new contributor might be.

" I'll call ; good morning, sir."

Following Mr. Dashwood's directions, and making Mrs. Northbury her model, Jo rashly took a plunge into the frothy sea of sensational literature. She sincerely meant to write nothing of which she should be ashamed, and quieted all pricks of conscience by anticipations of the happy minute when she should show her earnings and laugh over her well-kept secret. But Mr. Dashwood rejected any except thrilling tales ; and so history and romance, land and sea, science and art, police records and lunatic asylums, had to be ransacked for the purpose. Eager to find material for stories, and bent on making them original in plot, if not masterly in execution, she searched newspapers for accidents, incidents, and crimes, and introduced herself to folly, sin and misery, as well as her limited opportunities allowed. She was living in bad society, imaginary though it was, for she was feeding heart and fancy on dangerous food, and was fast brushing the innocent bloom from her nature by a premature acquaintance with the darker side of life, which comes soon enough to all of us.

I don't know whether the study of Shakespeare helped her to read character, or the natural instinct of a woman for what was honest, brave, and strong ; but while endowing her imaginary heroes with every perfection under the sun, Jo was discovering a live hero, who interested her in spite of many human imperfections. Mr. Bhaer, in one of their conversations, had advised her to study simple, true, and lovely characters, wherever she found them, as good training for a writer ; Jo took him at his word,—for she coolly turned round and studied him,—a proceeding which would have much surprised him, had he known it, —for the worthy Professor was very humble in his own conceit.

Why everybody liked him was what puzzled Jo, at first. He was neither rich nor great, young nor handsome, in no respect what is called fascinating, imposing, or brilliant ; and yet he was as attractive as a genial fire, and people seemed to gather about him as naturally as about a warm hearth.

" That's it ! " said Jo to herself, when she at length discovered that genuine good-will towards one's fellow-men could dignify even a stout German teacher, who darned his own socks, and was burdened with the name of Bhaer.

Jo valued goodness highly, but she also possessed a most feminine respect for intellect, and a little discovery which she made about the Professor, added much to her regard for him. He never spoke of himself, and no one knew, till a fellow-countryman came to see him, and divulged the pleasing fact that he was an honoured professor in Berlin, though only a poor language-master in America, and his homely, hardworking life was much beautified by the spice of romance which this discovery gave it. She valued his esteem, she coveted his respect, she wanted to be worthy of his friendship; and, just when the wish was sincerest, she came near losing everything. It all grew out of a cocked hat; for one evening the Professor came in to give Jo her lesson, with a paper soldier-cap on his head, which Tina had put there, and he had forgotten to take off.

" It's evident he doesn't prink at his glass before coming down," thought Jo, with a smile, as he said " Goot efening," and sat soberly down, quite unconscious of the ludicrous contrast between his subject and his head-gear, for he was going to read her the " Death of Wallenstein."

She liked to hear him laugh out his big, hearty laugh, when anything funny happened, so she left him to discover it for himself, and presently forgot all about it; for to hear a German read Schiller is rather an absorbing occupation. After the reading came the lesson, which was a lively one, for the cocked-hat kept her eyes dancing with merriment. The Professor didn't know what to make of her, and stopped, at last, to ask with mild surprise,—

" Mees Marsch, for what do you laugh in your master's face? Haf you no respect for me, that you go on so bad?"

" How can I be respectful, when you, sir, forget to take your hat off?" said Jo.

Lifting his hand to his head, the Professor gravely felt and removed the little cocked-hat, looked at it, and then threw back his head, and laughed like a merry bass-viol.

" Ah! I see him now; it is that imp Tina who makes me a fool with my cap. Well, see you, if this lesson goes not well, you too shall wear him."

But the lesson did not go at all, for a few minutes, because Mr. Bhaer caught sight of a picture on the hat; and unfolding it, said with an air of great disgust,—

" I wish these papers did not come in the house ; they are not for young people to read. I haf no patience with those who make this harm."

Jo glanced at the sheet, and saw a pleasing illustration, composed of a lunatic, a corpse, a villain, and a viper. She did not like it ; but the impulse that made her turn it over was not one of displeasure, but fear, because, for a minute, she fancied the paper was the *Volcano.* It was not, however, and her panic subsided as she remembered that, even if it had been, and one of her own tales in it, there would have been no name to betray her. She had betrayed herself, however, by a look and a blush ; for, though an absent man, the Professor saw a good dea more than people fancied.

" I would more rather give my boys gunpowder to play with than this bad trash," he continued earnestly.

" All may not be bad—only silly, you know ; and if there is a demand for it, I don't see any harm in supplying it. Many respectable people make an honest living out of what are called sensational stories," said Jo, scratching gathers energetically.

" There is a demand for whisky, but I think you and I do not care to sell it. If the respectable people knew what harm they did, they would not feel that the living *was* honest. They haf no right to put poison in the sugar-plum, and let the small ones eat it. No ; they should think a little, and sweep mud in the street before they do this thing ! "

Mr. Bhaer spoke warmly, and walked to the fire, crumpling the paper in his hands. Jo sat still, looking as if the fire had come to her ; for her cheeks burned long after the cocked-hat had turned to smoke, and gone harmlessly up the chimney. Then she thought con-solingly to herself, " Mine are not like that ; they are only silly, never bad ; so I won't be worried ; " and taking up her book, she said, with a studious face,—

" Shall we go on ? I'll be very good and proper now.

" I shall hope so," was all he said, but the grave, kind look he gave her, made her feel as if the words *Weekly Volcano* were printed in large type on her forehead.

As soon as she went to her room, she got out her papers, and carefully re-read every one of her stories.

" They *are* trash, for each is more sensational than the

last.—I know it's so—for I can't read this stuff in sober
earnest without being horribly ashamed of it ; and *what
should* I do if they were seen at home, or Mr. Bhaer got
hold of them ? "

Jo turned hot at the bare idea, and stuffed the whole
bundle into her stove, nearly setting the chimney afire
with the blaze. But when nothing remained of all her
three months' work, except a heap of ashes, and the money
in her lap, Jo sat on the floor, wondering what she ought
to do about her wages.

" I think I haven't done much harm *yet*, and may keep
this to pay for my time," she said, after a long meditation,
adding, impatiently, " I almost wish I hadn't any
conscience, it's so inconvenient."

Jo wrote no more sensational stories, deciding that the
money did not pay for her share of the sensation ; but,
going to the other extreme, as is the way with people of
her stamp, she took a course of Mrs. Sherwood, Miss
Edgeworth, and Hannah More ; and then produced a tale
which might have been more properly called an essay or a
sermon, so intensely moral was it. She sent this didactic
gem to several markets, but it found no purchaser ; and
she was inclined to agree with Mr. Dashwood, that morals
didn't sell.

Then she tried a child's story, which she could easily
have disposed of if she had not been mercenary enough to
demand filthy lucre for it. So nothing came of these
trials ; and Jo corked up her inkstand, and said, in a fit
of very wholesome humility,—

" I don't know anything ; I'll wait till I do before I try
again, and, meantime, ' sweep mud in the street,' if I can't
do better—that's honest, any way ; " which decision
proved that her second tumble down the bean-stalk had
done her some good.

While these internal revolutions were going on, her
external life had been as busy and uneventful as usual ;
and if she sometimes looked serious, or a little sad, no one
observed it but Professor Bhaer. He did it so quietly,
that Jo never knew he was watching to see if she would
accept and profit by his reproof ; but she stood the test,
and he was satisfied ; for, though no words passed between
them, he knew that she had given up writing.

It was a pleasant winter and a long one, for she did not

leave Mrs. Kirke till June. Everyone seemed sorry when
the time came; the children were inconsolable, and
Mr. Bhaer's hair stuck straight up all over his head—for
he always rumpled it wildly when disturbed in mind.

"Going home! Ah, you are happy that you haf a home
to go in," he said when she bade them all good-bye.

"Now, sir, you won't forget to come and see us, if you
ever travel our way, will you? I want them all to know
my friend," she said warmly.

"Do you? Shall I come?" he asked, looking down
at her with an eager expression, which she did not see.

"Yes, come next month; Laurie graduates then, and
you'd enjoy Commencement as something new."

"That is your best friend, of whom you speak?" he
said, in an altered tone.

"Yes, my boy Teddy; I'm very fond of him, and
should like you to see him."

Jo looked up, then, quite unconscious of anything but
her own pleasure, in the prospect of showing them to one
another. Something in Mr. Bhaer's face suddenly recalled
the fact that she might find Laurie more than a best friend,
and she involuntarily began to blush. Fortunately, the
child on her knee was moved to hug her; so she managed
to hide her face for an instant, hoping the Professor did not
see it. But he did, and his own changed again from that
momentary anxiety to its usual expression, as he said,
cordially—

"I fear I shall not make the time for that, but I wish
the friend much success, and you all happiness; Gott
bless you!" and with that he shook hands warmly, and
went away.

But after the boys were abed, he sat long before his fire,
with a tired look on his face. Once when he remembered
Jo, as she sat with the little child in her lap, and that new
softness in her face, he leaned his head on his hands a
minute. "It is not for me; I must not hope it now," he
said to himself, with a sigh that was almost a groan; then
as if reproaching himself for the longing that he could not
repress, he went and kissed the two towzled heads upon
the pillow, took down his seldom-used meerschaum, and
opened his Plato.

CHAPTER XII

HEARTACHE

WHATEVER his motive might have been, Laurie graduated with honour, and gave the Latin oration with grace and eloquence—so his friends said. They were all there—his grandfather, oh, so proud ! Mr. and Mrs. March, John and Meg, Jo and Beth, and all exulted over him with the sincere admiration which boys make light of at the time, but fail to win from the world by any after-triumphs.

" I've got to stay for this confounded supper,—but I shall be home to-morrow ; you'll come and meet me, girls ? " Laurie said, as he put the sisters into the carriage after the joys of the day were over. He said " girls," but he meant Jo,—and she had not the heart to refuse, but answered, warmly,—

" I'll come, Teddy, rain or shine, and march before you, playing *Hail the conquering hero comes*, on a jew's-harp."

Laurie thanked her with a look that made her think, " Oh, dear ! I know he'll say something ; what shall I do ? "

" Where's the jew's-harp, Jo ? " cried Laurie next day, as soon as he was within speaking distance.

" I forgot it ; " and Jo took heart again, for that salutation could not be called lover-like.

She always used to take his arm on these occasions ; now she did not, and he made no complaint, but talked on rapidly about all sorts of far-away subjects, till they turned into the little path that led homeward. Then he walked slowly, and a dreadful pause occurred. To rescue the conversation from the wells of silence into which it kept falling, Jo said, hastily,—

" Now you must have a good, long holiday ! "

" I intend to."

Something in his resolute tone made Jo look up quickly, to find him looking down at her with an expression that assured her the dreaded moment had come, and made her put out her hand with an imploring,

" No, Teddy,—please don't ! "

" I will ; and you *must* hear me. It's no use, Jo, we've got to have it out, and the sooner the better for both of us," he answered, getting flushed and excited all at once.

" Say what you like, then," said Jo, desperately.

Laurie was a young lover, but he was in earnest, so he plunged into the subject with characteristic impetuosity, saying, in a voice that *would* get choky now and then, in spite of manful efforts to keep it steady,—

" I've loved you ever since I've known you, Jo. I've tried to show it, but you wouldn't let me ; now I'm going to make you hear, and give me an answer, for I *can't* go on so any longer."

" I wanted to save you this ; I thought you'd understand—" began Jo, finding it a great deal harder than she expected.

" I know you did ; but girls are so queer. They say No, when they mean Yes ; and drive a man out of his wits just for the fun of it," returned Laurie.

" *I* don't. I never wanted to make you care for me so, and I went away to keep you from it if I could."

" I thought so ; it was like you, but it was no use. I only loved you all the more, and I worked hard to please you, and I gave up billiards and everything you didn't like, for I hoped you'd love me, though I'm not half good enough."

" Yes, you are ; you're a great deal too good for me, and I'm so proud and fond of you, I don't see why I can't love you as you want me to. I've tried, but I can't change the feeling, and it would be a lie to say I do when I don't."

" Really, truly, Jo ? "

He stopped short, and caught both her hands as he put his question, with a look that she did not soon forget.

" Really, truly, dear ? "

They were in the grove now,—close by the stile ; and when the last words fell reluctantly from Jo's lips, Laurie dropped her hands and turned as if to go on, but for once in his life that fence was too much for him ; so he just laid his head down on the mossy post, and stood so still that Jo was frightened.

" Oh, Teddy, I'm so sorry, so desperately sorry, I could kill myself if it would do any good ! But you know it's impossible for people to make themselves love other people if they don't," cried Jo, remorsefully, as she patted his shoulder, remembering the time when he had comforted her so long ago.

"They do sometimes," said a muffled voice from the post.

"I don't believe it's the right sort of love, and I'd rather not try it," was the decided answer. "I agree with mother, that you and I are not suited to each other, because our quick tempers and strong wills would probably make us very miserable, if we were so foolish as to—" Jo paused a little over the last word, but Laurie uttered it with a rapturous expression,—

"Marry, no we shouldn't! If you loved me, Jo, I should be a perfect saint,—for you can make me anything you like!"

"No I can't. I've tried it and failed, and I won't risk our happiness by such a serious experiment. We don't agree, and we never shall; so we'll be good friends all our lives, but we won't go and do anything rash."

"Yes, we will if we get the chance," muttered Laurie, rebelliously.

"Now do be reasonable, and take a sensible view of the case," implored Jo, almost at her wit's end.

"I won't be reasonable; I don't want to take what you call 'a sensible view;' it won't help me, and it only makes you harder. I don't believe you've got any heart."

"I wish I hadn't!"

There was a little quiver in Jo's voice, and, thinking it a good omen, Laurie turned round, bringing all his persuasive powers to bear as he said, in the wheedlesome tone that had never been so dangerously wheedlesome before,—

"Don't disappoint us, dear! everyone expects it. Grandpa has set his heart upon it,—your people like it,— and I can't get on without you. Say you will, and let's be happy! do, do!"

Not until months afterward did Jo understand how she had the strength of mind to hold fast to the resolution she had made when she decided that she did not love her boy, and never could. It was very hard to do, but she did it, knowing that delay was both useless and cruel.

"I can't say 'Yes' truly, so I won't say it at all. I've done my best, but you *won't* be reasonable, and it's selfish

of you to keep teasing for what I can't give. I shall always
be fond of you,—very fond indeed, as a friend,—but I'll
never marry you ; and the sooner you believe it the better
for both of us,—so now."

That speech was like fire to gunpowder. Laurie looked
at her a minute, as if he did not quite know what to do
with himself, then turned sharply away, saying, in a
desperate sort of tone,—

" You'll be sorry, some day, Jo."

" Oh, where are you going ? " she cried, for his face
frightened her.

" To the devil ! " was the consoling answer.

For a minute Jo's heart stood still, as he swung himself
down the bank, toward the river ; but it takes much folly,
sin, or misery to send a young man to a violent death,
and Laurie was not one of the weak sort. Some blind
instinct led him to fling hat and coat into his boat, and
row away with all his might, making better time up the
river than he had done in many a race. Jo drew a long
breath, as she watched the poor fellow trying to outstrip
the trouble in his heart.

" That will do him good, and he'll come home in such a
penitent state of mind, that I shan't dare to see him," she
said ; adding, as she went slowly home, feeling as if she
had murdered some innocent thing,—" Now I must go and
prepare Mr. Laurence to be very kind to my poor boy.
I wish he'd love Beth ; perhaps he may, in time, but
I begin to think I was mistaken about her. Oh dear ! how
can girls like to have lovers and refuse them. I think
it's dreadful."

Being sure that no one could do it as well as herself, she
went straight to Mr. Laurence, told the hard story bravely
through, and then broke down, crying so dismally over her
own insensibility, that the kind old gentleman, though
sorely disappointed, did not utter a reproach. When
Laurie came home, dead tired, but quite composed, he
went to his piano, and began to play. The windows were
open ; and Jo, walking in the garden with Beth, for once
understood music better than her sister, for he played the
" Sonata Pathetique," and played it as he never did
before.

" That's very fine, I dare say, but it's sad enough to
make one cry ; give us something gayer, lad," said **Mr.**

Laurence, whose kind old heart was full of sympathy, which he longed to show, but knew not how.

Laurie dashed into a livelier strain and would have got through bravely, if, in a momentary lull, Mrs. March's voice had not been heard calling,—

" Jo, dear, come in ; I want you."

Just what Laurie longed to say, with a different meaning ! As he listened, he lost his place ; the music ended with a broken chord, and the musician sat silent in the dark.

" I can't stand this," muttered the old gentleman,—up he got, groped his way to the piano, laid a kind hand on either of the broad shoulders, and said, as gently as a woman,—

" I know, my boy, I know."

No answer for an instant ; then Laurie asked, sharply,—

" Who told you ? "

" Jo herself."

" Then there's an end of it ! " and he shook off his grandfather's hands with an impatient motion ; for though grateful for the sympathy, his man's pride could not bear a man's pity.

" Not quite ; I want to say one thing, and then there shall be an end of it," returned Mr. Laurence, with unusual mildness. " You won't care to stay at home, just now, perhaps ? "

" I don't intend to run away from a girl. Jo can't prevent my seeing her, and I shall stay and do it as long as I like," interrupted Laurie, in a defiant tone.

" Not if you are the gentleman I think you. I'm dis-appointed, but the girl can't help it ; and the only thing left for you is to go away for a time. Why not go abroad, as you planned, and forget it ? "

" I can't."

" But you've been wild to go, and I promised you should, when you got through college."

" Ah, but I didn't mean to go alone ! "

" I don't ask you to go alone ; there's someone ready and glad to go with you, anywhere in the world."

" Who, sir ? "

" Myself."

Laurie put out his hand, saying huskily,—

" I'm a selfish brute ; but—you know—grandfather—"

" Lord help me, yes, I do know, for I've been through

F

it all before in my own young days. Now, my dear boy, just sit quietly down, and hear my plan."

" Well, sir, what is it ? " and Laurie sat down without a sign of interest in face or voice.

" There is business in London that needs looking after ; I meant you should attend to it ; but I can do it better myself, and things here will get on very well with Brooke to manage them."

" But you hate travelling, sir ; I can't ask it of you at your age," began Laurie, who was grateful, but much preferred to go alone.

The old gentleman knew that perfectly well, and particularly desired to prevent it, sure that it would not be wise to leave him to his own devices. So, stifling a natural regret at the thought of the home comforts he would leave behind him, he said, stoutly,—

" Bless your soul, I'm not superannuated yet. I quite enjoy the idea ; it will do me good, for travelling now-a-days is almost as easy as sitting in a chair,"

A restless movement from Laurie made the old man add, hastily,—

" I don't mean to be a marplot or to gad about with you, but leave you free to go where you like, while I amuse myself in my own way. I've friends in London and Paris, and should like to visit them ; meantime, you can go to Italy, and enjoy pictures, music, scenery and adventures, to your heart's content."

Now, Laurie felt just then that his heart was entirely broken, but at the sound of certain words which the old gentleman artfully introduced into his sentence, the broken heart gave an unexpected leap, and he sighed, saying in a spiritless tone,—

" Just as you like, sir ; it doesn't matter what I do."

" It does to me—remember that, my lad ; I give you entire liberty, but I trust you to make an honest use of it. Promise me that, Laurie."

" Anything you like, sir."

" Good ! " thought the old gentleman ; " you don't care now, but there'll come a time when that promise will keep you out of mischief, or I'm much mistaken."

Being an energetic individual, Mr. Laurence struck while the iron was hot ; and before the blighted being recovered spirit enough to rebel, they were off.

When the parting came, Laurie affected high spirits, to conceal certain inconvenient emotions which seemed inclined to assert themselves, and he got on very well till Jo followed to wave her hand to him if he looked round. He did look round, came back, put his arms about her as she stood on the step above him, and looked up at her with a face that made his short appeal both eloquent and pathetic.

" Oh, Jo, can't you ? "

" Teddy, dear, I wish I could ! "

That was all, except a little pause ; then Laurie straightened himself up, " It's all right, never mind," and went away without another word.   Ah, but it wasn't all right, and Jo *did* mind ; for when he left her, without a look behind him, she knew that the boy Laurie never would come again.

CHAPTER XIII

BETH'S SECRET

WHEN Jo came home that spring, she had been struck with the change in Beth.   No one seemed aware of it, for it had come too gradually to startle those who saw her daily ; and presently, in other cares, Jo for a time forgot her fear.

But when Laurie was gone, and peace prevailed again, the vague anxiety returned and haunted her.   She had confessed her sins and been forgiven ; but when she showed her savings and proposed the mountain trip, Beth had thanked her heartily, but begged not to go so far away from home.   Another little visit to the seashore would suit her better, and Jo took Beth down to a quiet place, where she could let the fresh sea breezes blow a little colour into her pale cheeks.

It was not a fashionable place, but even among the pleasant people there, the girls made few friends preferring to live for one another. Beth was too shy to enjoy society, and Jo too wrapt up in her to care for anyone else ; so they were all in all to each other, and came and went, quite unconscious of the interest they excited in those about them,—who watched with sympathetic eyes the strong sister and the feeble one, always together, as if they felt instinctively that a long separation was not far away.

One day Beth told her. Jo thought she was asleep, she lay so still ; and, putting down her book, sat looking at her with wistful eyes,—trying to see signs of hope in the faint colour on Beth's cheeks. But she could not find enough to satisfy her,—for the cheeks were very thin and the hands seemed too feeble to hold even the rosy little shells they had been gathering. For a minute her eyes were too dim for seeing, and, when they cleared, Beth was looking up at her so tenderly, that there was hardly any need for her to say,—

" Jo, dear, I'm glad you know it. I've tried to tell you, but I couldn't."

There was no answer except her sister's cheek against her own,—not even tears,—for when most deeply moved Jo did not cry.

" I've known it for a good while, dear, and now I'm used to it, it isn't hard to think of or to bear."

" Is this what made you so unhappy in the autumn, Beth ? " asked Jo.

" Yes ; I gave up hoping then, but I didn't like to own it ; I tried to think it was a sick fancy, and would not let it trouble anyone. But when I saw you all so well and strong, and full of happy plans, it was hard to feel that I could never be like you,—and then I was miserable, Jo."

" Oh, Beth, and you didn't tell me ! How could you shut me out, and bear it all alone ? "

Jo's voice was full of tender reproach, and her heart ached to think of the solitary struggle that must have gone on while Beth learned to say good-bye to health, love, and life, and take up her cross so cheerfully.

" Perhaps it was wrong, but I wasn't sure, and I hoped I was mistaken. It would have been selfish to frighten you all when Marmee was so anxious about Meg, and Amy away, and you so happy with Laurie,—at least, I thought so then."

" And I thought that you loved him, Beth, and I went away because I couldn't," cried Jo,—glad to say all the truth.

Beth looked so amazed at the idea, that Jo smiled in spite of her pain, and added softly,—

" Then you didn't, deary ? I was afraid it was so, and imagined your poor little heart full of love-lornity all that while."

" Why, Jo ! how could I, when he was so fond of you ? " asked Beth, as innocently as a child. " I do love him ; he is so good to me. But he never could be anything but my brother. I hope he will be, some time."

" Not through me," said Jo, decidedly. " Amy is left for him, and they would suit excellently,—but I have no heart for such things now, Beth. You *must* get well."

" I want to,—oh, so much ! I try, but every day I lose a little. It's like the tide, Jo, when it turns,—it goes slowly, but it can't be stopped."

" It *shall* be stopped,—your tide must not turn so soon, —nineteen is too young. Beth, I can't let you go. I'll work, and pray, and fight against it. God won't be so cruel as to take you from me," cried poor Jo, rebelliously.

Simple, sincere people seldom speak much of their piety ; Beth could not explain the faith that gave her courage to give up life, and cheerfully wait for death. She did not rebuke Jo with saintly speeches, only loved her better for her passionate affection. She could not say, " I'm glad to go," for life was very sweet to her ; she could only sob out, " I'll try to be willing," while she held fast to Jo, as the first bitter wave of this great sorrow broke over them together.

By-and-by, Beth said, with recovered serenity—

" You'll tell them this, when we go home ? "

" I think they will see it without words," sighed Jo ; for now it seemed to her that Beth changed every day.

" Perhaps not ; I've heard that the people who love best are often blindest to such things. If they don't see it, you will tell them for me, won't you, Jo ? "

" Beth, I don't give up yet ; I'm going to believe that it *is* a sick fancy, and not let you think it's true," said Jo, trying to speak cheerfully.

Beth lay a minute thinking, and then said in her quiet way,—

" I don't know how to express myself. But I have a feeling that it was never intended I should live long. I never made any plans about what I'd do when I grew up ; I never thought of being married, as you all did. I never wanted to go away, and the hard part now is the leaving you all. I'm not afraid, but it seems as if I should be homesick for you, even in heaven."

Jo could not speak ; and for several minutes there was no sound but the sigh of the wind, and the lapping of the tide. A white-winged gull flew by, with the flash of sunshine on its silvery breast ; Beth watched it till it vanished, and her eyes were full of sadness.

" You are like the gull, Jo, strong and wild, fond of the storm and the wind, flying far out to sea, and happy all alone. Meg is the turtledove, and Amy is like the lark she writes about, trying to get up among the clouds, but always dropping down into its nest again. I hope I shall see her again, but she seems *so* far away."

" She is coming in the spring, and I mean to have you well and rosy, by that time," began Jo, feeling that of all the changes in Beth, the talking change was the greatest, for she thought aloud in a quiet way unlike bashful Beth.

" Jo, dear, don't hope any more ; it won't do any good, I'm sure of that. We'll have happy times, for I don't suffer much, and I think the tide will go out easily, if you help me."

Jo leaned down to kiss the tranquil face ; and with that silent kiss she dedicated herself soul and body to Beth.

She was right,—there was no need of any words when they got home, for father and mother saw plainly, now, what they had prayed to be saved from seeing. Tired with her short journey, Beth went at once to bed, and when Jo went down, she found that she would be spared the hard task of telling Beth's secret. Her father stood leaning his head on the mantelpiece, and did not turn as she came in ; but her mother stretched out her arms as if for help, and Jo went to comfort her without a word.

CHAPTER XIV

NEW IMPRESSIONS

AT three o'clock in the afternoon, all the fashionable world at Nice may be seen on the Promenade des Anglais,—a charming place ; bordered with palms, flowers, and tropical shrubs, bounded on one side by the sea, on the other by the grand drive, lined with hotels and villas, while beyond lie orange orchards and the hills. Along this walk, on Christmas day, a tall young man strolled slowly, with his hands behind him, and a somewhat absent expression of countenance. There were plenty of pretty faces to admire, but the young man took little notice of them, except to glance now and then at some blonde girl, or lady in blue. Presently he strolled out of the promenade, and stood a moment at the crossing, as if undecided whether to go and listen to the band in the Jardin Publique, or to wander along the beach toward Castle Hill. The quick trot of ponies' feet made him look up, as one of the little carriages, containing a single lady, came rapidly down the street. The lady was young, blonde, and dressed in blue. He stared a minute, then his whole face woke up, and, waving his hat like a boy, he hurried forward to meet her.

" Oh Laurie ! is it really you ? I thought you'd never come ! " cried Amy, dropping the reins, and holding out both hands to him.

" I was detained by the way, but I promised to spend Christmas with you, and here I am."

" How is your grandfather ? When did you come ? Where are you staying ? "

" Very well—last night—at the Chauvain. I called at your hotel, but you were all out."

" I have so much to say, and don't know where to begin. Get in, and we can talk at our ease ; I was going for a drive, and longing for company. Flo's saving up for to-night."

" What happens then—a ball ? "

"A Christmas party at our hotel. There are many Americans there, and they give it in honour of the day. You'll go with us, of course ? Aunt will be charmed."

"Thank you ! where now ? " asked Laurie, leaning back and folding his arms, a proceeding which suited Amy, who preferred to drive ; for her parasol whip and blue reins, over the white ponies' backs afforded her infinite satisfaction.

"I'm going to the banker's first, for letters, and then to Castle Hill ; the view is lovely. Have you ever been there ? "

"Often, years ago ; but I don't mind having a look at it."

"Now tell me all about yourself. The last I heard of you, your grandfather wrote that he expected you from Berlin."

"Yes, I spent a month there, and then joined him in Paris, where he has settled for the winter. He has friends there, and finds plenty to amuse him ; so we get on capitally."

"That's a sociable arrangement," said Amy, missing something in Laurie's manner, though she couldn't tell what.

"Why, you see he hates to travel, and I hate to keep still : so we each suit ourselves, and there is no trouble. I am often with him, and he enjoys my adventures while I like to feel that someone is glad to see me when I get back from my wanderings. Dirty old hole, isn't it ? " he added, with a sniff of disgust, as they drove along the boulevard to the Place Napoleon.

"The dirt is picturesque, so I don't mind. The river and the hills are delicious, and these glimpses of the narrow cross streets are my delight. Now we shall have to wait for that procession to pass ; it's going to the church of St. John."

While Laurie listlessly watched the procession of priests and some brotherhood in blue, chanting as they walked, Amy watched him, and felt a new sort of shyness steal over her, for he was changed, and she couldn't find the merry-faced boy she left, in the moody-looking man beside her. He was handsomer than ever, she thought; but looked tired and spiritless. She couldn't understand it, and did not venture to ask questions ; so she touched up her ponies, as the procession wound away across the arches of the Paglioni bridge.

At Avigdor's she found the precious home-letters, and, giving the reins to Laurie, read them luxuriously as they wound up the shady road between green hedges, where tea-roses blossomed.

"Beth is very poorly, mother says. I often think I ought to go home, but they all say, 'stay'; so I do, for I shall never have another chance like this," said Amy, looking sober over one page.

"I think you are right, there; you could do nothing at home, and it is a great comfort to them to know that you are well and happy, and enjoying so much, my dear."

He looked more like his old self, as he said that; and the fear that sometimes weighed on Amy's heart was lightened, —for the brotherly "my dear," seemed to assure her that if any trouble did come, she would not be alone in a strange land. Presently she laughed and showed him a small sketch of Jo in her scribbling suit, with the bow rampantly erect upon her cap, and issuing from her mouth the words, "Genius burns!"

Laurie put it in his vest pocket "to keep it from blowing away," and listened with interest to the letter Amy read him.

"This will be a regularly merry Christmas to me, with presents in the morning, you and letters in the afternoon, and a party at night," said Amy, as they alighted among the ruins of the old fort, and a flock of peacocks came trooping about them. While Amy scattered crumbs to the brilliant birds, Laurie looked at her as she had looked at him with a natural curiosity to see what changes time and absence had wrought. He found nothing to disappoint, much to admire and interest him, and carried away a pretty picture of a bright-faced girl standing in the sunshine, which brought out the fresh colour of her cheeks, the golden gloss of her hair, and made her a prominent figure in the pleasant scene.

As they came up the hill, Amy waved her hand as if welcoming him to her favourite haunt, and said,—

"Do you remember the Cathedral and the Corso, and that speck far out to sea which they say is Corsica?"

"I remember," he answered, without enthusiasm.

"What Jo would give for a sight of that famous speck!" said Amy, feeling in good spirits, and anxious to see him so also.

"Yes," was all he said, but he turned his eyes to the island.

"Take a good look at it for her sake, and then come and tell me what you have been doing with yourself all this while," said Amy, seating herself, ready for a good talk.

But she did not get it ; for, though he answered all her questions freely, she could only learn that he had roved about the Continent and been to Greece. So, after idling away an hour, they drove home again ; and, having paid his respects to Mrs. Carrol, Laurie left them, promising to return in the evening.

It must be recorded of Amy, that she deliberately "prinked" that night. Tarlatan and tulle were cheap at Nice, so she enveloped herself in them on such occasions, and, following the sensible English fashion of simple dress for young girls, got up charming little toilettes with fresh flowers, a few trinkets, and all manner of dainty devices, which were both inexpensive and effective.

"I do want him to think I look well, and tell them so at home," said Amy to herself, as she put on Flo's old white silk ball dress, and covered it with a cloud of fresh illusion, out of which her white shoulders and golden head emerged with a most artistic effect. Her hair she had the sense to let alone, gathering up the thick waves into a Hebe-like knot at the back of her head.

"My new fan just matches my flowers, and the real lace on aunt's *mouchoir* gives an air to my whole dress. If I only had a classical nose and mouth I should be happy," she said, surveying herself with a critical eye.

In spite of this affliction, she looked unusually gay and graceful as she walked up and down the long saloon while waiting for Laurie, who came in so quietly that she did not hear him ; and, as she stood at the distant window with her head half turned, the slender, white figure against the red curtains was as effective as a well-placed statue.

"Good evening, Diana!" said Laurie, with the look of satisfaction she liked to see in his eyes when they rested on her.

"Good evening, Apollo!" she answered, smiling back at him—and the thought of entering the ball-room on the arm of such a personable man caused Amy to pity the four plain Misses Davis from the bottom of her heart.

"Here are your flowers!" said Laurie, handing her a delicate nosegay, in a holder that she had long coveted as she daily passed it in Cardiglia's window.

" How kind you are ! " she exclaimed, gratefully ; " if I'd known you were coming I'd have had something ready for you to-day,—though not as pretty as this, I'm afraid."

" Thank you ; it isn't what it should be, but you have improved it," he added, as she snapped the silver bracelet on her wrist.

" Please, don't ! "

" I thought you liked that sort of thing ! "

" Not from you ; it doesn't sound natural, and I like your old bluntness better."

" I'm glad of it ! " he answered, with a look of relief ; then buttoned her gloves for her, and asked if his tie was straight, just as he used to do when they went to parties together at home.

The company assembled in the long *salle à manger*, that evening, was such as one sees nowhere but on the Continent. The hospitable Americans had invited every acquaintance they had in Nice, and, having no prejudice against titles, secured a few to add lustre to their Christmas ball.

Any young girl can imagine Amy's state of mind when she " took the stage " that night, leaning on Laurie's arm. She knew she looked well, she loved to dance, she felt that her foot was on her native heath in a ballroom, and enjoyed the delightful sense of power which comes when young girls first discover the new and lovely kingdom they are born to rule by virtue of beauty, youth, and womanhood. With the first burst of the band, Amy's colour rose, her eyes began to sparkle, and her feet to tap the floor impatiently ; therefore the shock she received can better be imagined than described, when he said, in a perfectly tranquil tone,—

" Do you care to dance ? "

" One usually does at a ball ! "

Her amazed look caused Laurie to repair his error as fast as possible.

" I meant the first dance. May I have the honour ? "

" I can give you one if I put off the Count. He dances divinely ; but he will excuse me, as you are an old friend," said Amy, hoping that the name would have a good effect.

" Nice little boy, but rather a short Pole to support the steps of

'A daughter of the gods Divinely tall, and more divinely fair,'

was all the satisfaction she got, however.

The set in which they found themselves was composed of English, and Amy was compelled to step decorously through a slow measure, feeling all the while as if she could dance the Tarantella with a relish. Laurie resigned her to the "nice little boy," and went to do his duty to Flo, without securing Amy for the joys to come, which reprehensible want of forethought was properly punished, for she immediately engaged herself till supper, meaning to relent if he then gave sign of penitence. She showed him her ball-book with demure satisfaction when he strolled up to claim her ; but his polite regrets didn't impose upon her, and when she galloped away with the Count, she saw Laurie sit down by her aunt, with an actual expression of relief.

That was unpardonable ; and Amy took no more notice of him for a long while, except a word now and then, when she came to her chaperon, between the dances, for a necessary pin or a moment's rest. When little Vladimir finally relinquished her, with assurances that he was "desolated to leave so early," she was ready to rest, and see how her recreant knight had borne his punishment.

It had been successful ; for, at three-and-twenty, blighted affections find a balm in friendly society, and young spirits rise, when subjected to the enchantment of beauty, music and motion. Laurie had a waked-up look as he rose to give her his seat ; and when he hurried away to bring her some supper, she said to herself, with a satisfied smile, —

"Ah, I thought that would do him good ! "

"You look like Balzac's *Femme peinte par elle-mêne*," he said, as he fanned her.

"My rouge won't come off " ; and Amy rubbed her brilliant cheek, and showed him her white glove, with a simplicity that made him laugh outright.

"What do you call this stuff ? " he asked, touching a fold of her dress that had blown over his knee.

"Illusion."

"Good name for it ; it's very pretty—new thing, isn't it ? "

"It's as old as the hills ; you've seen it on dozens of girls, and you never found out that it was pretty till now— *stupide !* "

"I never saw it on you, before, which accounts for the mistake, you see."

" That is forbidden ; I'd rather take coffee than compliments, just now."

" Where did you learn all this sort of thing ? " he asked, with a quizzical look.

" As ' this sort of thing ' is rather a vague expression, would you kindly explain ? " returned Amy, wickedly leaving him to describe what is indescribable.

" Well—the general air, the style, the self-possession, the—the—illusion—you know," laughed Laurie, helping himself out of his quandary with the new word.

Amy was gratified, but demurely answered,—

" Foreign life polishes one in spite of one's self, and as for this "—with a little gesture toward her dress—" why, tulle is cheap ; posies to be had for nothing, and I am used to making the most of my poor little things."

Amy rather regretted that last sentence, fearing it wasn't in good taste ; but Laurie liked her the better for it, respecting the cheerful spirit that covered poverty with flowers. Amy did not know why he looked at her so kindly, and devoted himself to her for the rest of the evening, in the most delightful manner ; but the impulse that wrought this agreeable change was the result of one of the new impressions which both of them were unconsciously giving and receiving.

CHAPTER XV

ON THE SHELF

In France, the young girls have a dull time of it till they are married, when " *Vive la liberté*" becomes their motto. In America, as everyone knows, girls early sign a declaration of independence, and enjoy their freedom with republican zest ; but the young matrons usually abdicate with the first heir to the throne, and go into a seclusion also as close as a French nunnery, though by no means as quiet. Meg did not experience this affliction till her babies were a year old for she was a womanly little woman, the maternal instinct was very strong, and she was absorbed in her children, to the exclusion of everything else. Day and night she brooded over them with tireless devotion, leaving John to the tender mercies of the help. Being a domestic man, John missed the wifely attentions he had been accustomed to receive ; but, as he adored his babies, he cheerfully relinquished his comfort for a time, supposing, with masculine ignorance, that peace would soon be restored. But three months passed, and there was no return of repose ; Meg looked worn and nervous,—the babies absorbed every minute of her time,—the house was neglected,—and Kitty, the cook, who took life "aisy," kept him on short commons. His sleep was broken by infant wails and visions of a phantom figure pacing to and fro, in the watches of the night ; his meals were interrupted by the frequent flight of the presiding genius, if a muffled chirp sounded from the nest above ; and, when he read his paper of an evening, Demi's colic got into the shipping list, and Daisy's fall affected the price of stocks,—for Mrs. Brooke was only interested in domestic news.

He bore it very patiently for six months, and when no signs of amendment appeared, he did what other paternal exiles do,—tried to get a little comfort elsewhere. Scott had married and gone house-keeping not far off, and John fell into the way of running over for an hour or two of an evening. Mrs. Scott was a lively girl ; the parlour was bright and attractive, the chessboard ready, plenty of gay gossip, and a nice little supper set forth in tempting style.

Meg rather approved of the new arrangement at first, and found it a relief to know that John was having a good time instead of dozing in the parlour, or tramping about the house and waking the children. But by-and-by, when the teething worry was over, and the idols went to sleep at proper hours, she began to miss John, to find her work-basket dull company, when he was not sitting opposite in his old dressing-gown. She would not ask him to stay at home, but felt injured because he did not know that she wanted him without being told,—entirely forgetting the many evenings he had waited for her in vain. Not a word did she say, however, till her mother found her in tears one day, and insisted on knowing what the matter was,—for Meg's drooping spirits had not escaped her observation.

"I wouldn't tell anyone except you, mother; but if John goes on so much longer, I might as well be a widow," replied Mrs. Brooke, drying her tears on Daisy's bib, with an injured air.

"Goes on how, my dear?" asked her mother, anxiously.

"He's away all day, and at night he is continually going over to the Scotts. It isn't fair that I should have the hardest work and never any amusement. Men are very selfish, even the best of them."

"So are women; don't blame John till you see where you are wrong yourself."

"But it can't be right for him to neglect me."

"Don't you neglect him?"

"I don't see how."

"Let me show you. Did John ever neglect you, as you call it, when you made it a point to give him your society of an evening,—his only leisure time?"

"No; but I can't do it now, with two babies to tend."

"I think you could, dear; and I think you ought. May I speak quite freely, and will you remember that it's mother who blames as well as mother who sympathizes?"

"Indeed I will! Speak to me, as if I was little Meg again. I often feel as if I needed teaching more than ever, since these babies look to me for everything."

Meg drew her low chair beside her mother's, and the two women rocked and talked lovingly together.

"You have only made the mistake that most young wives make,—forgotten your duty to your husband in your love for your children. A very natural and forgivable mistake, Meg, but one that had better be remedied before you take to different ways. I've seen it for some weeks, but have not spoken, feeling sure that it would come right, in time."

"I'm afraid it won't. If I ask him to stay he'll think I'm jealous, and I wouldn't insult him by such an idea. He doesn't see that I want him, and I don't know how to tell him without words."

"Make it so pleasant he won't want to go away. My dear, it isn't home without you, and you are always in the nursery."

"Oughtn't I to be there?"

"Not all the time; you owe something to John as well as to the babies; don't shut him out of the nursery, but teach him how to help in it."

" You really think so, mother ? "

" I know it, Meg, for I've tried it ; and I seldom give advice unless I've proved its practicability. When you and Jo were little, I went on just as you do, feeling as if I didn't do my duty unless I devoted myself wholly to you. Poor father took to his books, and I struggled along as well as I could, but Jo was too much for me. You were poorly, and I worried about you till I fell sick myself. Then father came to the rescue and made himself so helpful that I saw my mistake, and never have been able to get on without him since. If I were you I'd let John have more to do with the management of Demi,—for the boy needs training, and it's none too soon to begin. Let Hannah come and help you ; she is a capital nurse, and you may trust the precious babies to her while you do more housework. Then I'd try to take an interest in whatever John likes, talk with him, and educate yourself to take your part in the world's work, for it all affects you and yours."

" John is so sensible, I'm afraid he'll think I'm stupid if I ask him questions about politics and things."

" I don't believe he would. Try it, and see if he doesn't find your society far more agreeable than Mrs. Scott's suppers."

" I will. Poor John ! I'm afraid I *have* neglected him sadly, but I thought I was right, and he never said anything."

" He tried not to be selfish, but he *has* felt rather forlorn, I fancy. This is just the time, Meg, when young married people are apt to grow apart, and the very time when they ought to be most together. Don't let John be a stranger to the babies, for through them you will learn to know and love one another as you should. Now, dear, think over mother's preachment, act upon it if it seems good, and God bless you all ! "

Meg did think it over, found it good, and resolved to try a social evening with John ; so she ordered a nice supper, dressed herself prettily, and put the children to bed early, that nothing should interfere with her experiment. But, unfortunately, Demi's most unconquerable prejudice was against going to bed, and poor Meg sang and rocked, told stories, and tried every sleep-provoking wile she could devise, but all in vain—the big eyes wouldn't shut ; and long after Daisy had gone to byelow, like the chubby little

... pausing on the terrace to enjoy the view ...

[*see page 103*

bunch of good nature she was, naughty Demi lay staring at the light, with the most wide-awake expression of countenance.

"Will Demi lie still, like a good boy, while mamma runs down and gives papa his tea?" asked Meg, as the hall door softly closed, and the well-known step went tip-toeing into the dining-room.

"Me has tea!" said Demi, preparing to join in the revel.

"No; but I'll save you some little cakies for breakfast, if you'll go bye-bye, like Daisy. Will you, lovey?"

"Iss!" and Demi shut his eyes tight, as if to catch sleep, and hurry the desired day.

Taking advantage of the propitious moment, Meg slipped away, and ran down to greet her husband with a smiling face, and the little blue bow in her hair, which was his especial admiration. He saw it at once, and said, with pleased surprise,—

"Why, little mother, how gay we are to-night. Is it a birthday anniversary, or anything?"

"No; I'm tired of being a dowdy, so I dressed up as a change. You always make yourself nice for table, no matter how tired you are; so why shouldn't I, when I have the time?"

"I do it out of respect for you, my dear," said John.

"Ditto, ditto, Mr. Brooke," laughed Meg, looking young and pretty again, as she nodded to him over the teapot.

"Well, it's altogether delightful, dear!" and John sipped his tea with an air of repose, which was of very short duration, however; for, as he put down his cup, the door-handle rattled and a little voice was heard, saying, impatiently—

"Opy doy; me's tummin!"

"It's that naughty boy; I told him to go to sleep alone, and here he is, getting his death a-cold pattering over that canvas," said Meg, answering the call.

"Mornin' now," announced Demi, in a joyful tone, as he entered, every curl bobbing gaily as he pranced about the table, eyeing the "cakies" with loving glances.

"No, it isn't morning yet; you must go to bed then you can have the cake with sugar on it."

"Me loves parpar," said the artful one, preparing to climb the paternal knee, and revel in forbidden joys. But John shook his head, and said to Meg—

G

"If you told him to stay up there, and go to sleep alone, make him do it, or he will never learn to mind you."

"Yes, of course; come, Demi!" and Meg led her son away, feeling a strong desire to spank the little marplot who hopped beside her, labouring under the delusion that the bribe was to be administered as soon as they reached the nursery.

Nor was he disappointed; for the short-sighted woman actually gave him a lump of sugar, tucked him into his bed, and forbade any more promenades till morning.

"Iss!" said Demi the perjured, blissfully sucking his sugar, and regarding his first attempt as eminently successful.

Meg returned to her place, and supper was progressing pleasantly, when the little ghost walked again, and exposed the maternal delinquencies, by boldly demanding—

"More sudar, marmar."

"Now this won't do," said John, hardening his heart against the engaging little sinner. "We shall never know any peace till that child learns to go to bed properly. You have made a slave of yourself long enough. Put him in his bed, and leave him, Meg."

"He won't stay there; he never does, unless I sit by him."

"I'll manage him. Demi, go upstairs and get into your bed, as mamma bids you."

"S'ant!" replied the young rebel, helping himself to the coveted "cakie," and beginning to eat the same with calm audacity.

"You must never say that to papa; I shall carry you if you don't go yourself."

"Go 'way; me don't love parpar," and Demi retired to his mother's skirts for protection.

But even that refuge proved unavailing, for he was delivered over to the enemy, with a "Be gentle with him, John," which struck the culprit with dismay. Bereft of his cake and borne away by a strong hand to that detested bed, poor Demi could not restrain his wrath; but kicked and screamed lustily all the way upstairs. The minute he was put into bed on one side, he rolled out at the other, and made for the door, only to be ignominiously caught up by the tail of his little toga, and put back again, which lively performance was kept up till the young man's strength gave out, when he devoted himself to roaring at the top of his voice. This vocal exercise usually conquered Meg ; but John sat as unmoved as the post, which is popularly believed to be deaf. This new order of things disgusted him, and he howled dismally for " marmar," till the plaintive wails went to Meg's heart and she ran up to say, beseechingly—

" Let me stay with him, he'll cry himself sick."

" No he won't, he's so tired he will soon drop off, and then he will understand that he has got to mind."

" He's my child, and I can't have his spirit broken by harshness."

" He's my child, and I won't have his temper spoilt by indulgence. Go down, my dear, and leave the boy to me."

When John spoke in that masterful tone, Meg always obeyed, and never regretted her docility.

" Please let me kiss him, once, John ? "

" Certainly ; Demi, say ' good-night ' to mamma, and let her go and rest, for she is tired with taking care of you all day."

Meg always insisted upon it, that the kiss won the victory ; for, after it was given, Demi sobbed more quietly, and lay still.

" Poor little man ! he's worn out with crying ; I'll cover him up, and then go and set Meg's heart at rest," thought John, creeping to the bedside, hoping to find his rebellious heir asleep.

But he wasn't ; for the moment his father peeped at him, Demi's eyes opened, and he put up his arms, saying, with a penitent hiccough, " Me's dood, now."

Sitting on the stairs, outside, Meg wondered at the long silence which followed the uproar ; and, after imagining all sorts of impossible accidents, she slipped into the room, to set her fears at rest. Demi lay fast asleep, cuddled close in the circle of his father's arm, and holding his father's finger, So held, John had waited patiently till the little hand relaxed its hold ; and, while waiting, had fallen asleep, more tired by that tussle with his little son than with his whole day's work.

As Meg stood watching the two faces on the pillow, she smiled to herself, and then slipped away saying, in a satisfied tone,—

" I never need fear that John will be too harsh with my

babies, he *does* know how to manage them, and Demi *is* getting too much for me."

When John came down at last, expecting to find a reproachful wife, he was agreeably surprised to find Meg placidly trimming a bonnet, and to be greeted with the request to read something about the election, if he was not too tired. John wisely asked no questions, knowing that Meg couldn't keep a secret to save her life, and therefore the clue would soon appear. He read a long debate with the most amiable readiness, and then explained it in his most lucid manner, while Meg tried to ask intelligent questions, and keep her thoughts from wandering from the state of the nation to the state of her bonnet. In her secret soul she decided that the mission of politicians seemed to be calling each other names; but when John paused, she said with what she thought diplomatic ambiguity,—

"Well, I really don't see what we are coming to."

John laughed, and watched her as she poised a preparation of tulle and flowers on her hand, and regarded it with the genuine interest which his harangue had failed to waken.

"She is trying to like politics for my sake, so I'll try and like millinery for hers—that's only fair," thought John, adding aloud,

"That's very pretty; is it what you call a breakfast cap?"

"My dear man, it's a bonnet—my very best theatre bonnet!"

"I beg your pardon; it was so very small, I naturally mistook it for one of the fly-away things you sometimes wear. How do you keep it on?"

"These bits of lace are fastened under the chin, with a rosebud, so"—and Meg illustrated by putting on the bonnet, and regarding him with an air of satisfaction.

"It's a love of a bonnet, but I prefer the face inside, for it looks young and happy again," and John kissed the smiling face, to the great detriment of the rosebud under the chin.

"I'm glad you like it, for I want you to take me to one of the new concerts some night; I really need some music to put me in tune. Will you, please?"

"Of course I will, with all my heart. You have been

shut up so long, it will do you no end of good, and I shall enjoy it, of all things. What put it into your head, little mother ? "

" Well, I had a talk with Marmee the other day, and told her how cross and out of sorts I felt, and she said I needed change, and less care ; so Hannah is to help me with the children, and I'm to see to things about the house more, and now and then have a little fun, just to keep me from getting to be an old woman before my time. I've neglected you shamefully lately, and I'm going to make home what it used to be, if I can."

Never mind what John said, or what a very narrow escape the little bonnet had from utter ruin ; all that we have any business to know, is that everyone was better for the division of labour system ; the children throve under the paternal rule, for accurate, steadfast John brought order and obedience into Babydom, while Meg recovered her spirits, and composed her nerves, by plenty of wholesome exercise, a little pleasure, and much confidential conversation with her sensible husband. The Scotts came to the Brookes now, and everyone found the little house a cheerful place, full of happiness, content, and family love ; even gay Sallie Moffat liked to go there. " It is always so quiet and pleasant here ; it does me good, Meg," she used to say, looking about her with wistful eyes, as if trying to discover the charm, that she might use it in her great house, full of splendid loneliness, for there were no riotous, sunny-faced babies there, and Ned lived in a world of his own, where there was no place for her.

This is the sort of shelf on which young wives and mothers may consent to be laid, safe from the restless fret and fever of the world, finding, as Meg found, that a woman's happiest kingdom is home, her highest honour the art of ruling it—not as a queen, but a wise wife and mother.

CHAPTER XVI

LAZY LAURENCE

LAURIE went to Nice intending to stay a week, and remained a month. He was tired of wandering about alone, and Amy's familiar presence seemed to give a homelike charm to the foreign scenes in which she bore a part. They naturally took comfort in each other's society, and were much together—riding, walking, dancing, or dawdling—for, at Nice, no one can be very industrious during the gay season. But, while apparently amusing themselves in the most careless fashion, they were half-consciously making discoveries and forming opinions about each other.

" All the rest have gone to Monaco for the day ; and I am going to Valrosa to sketch ; will you come ? " said Amy, as she joined Laurie one lovely day when he lounged in about noon.

" Well, yes ; but isn't it rather warm for a long walk ? " he answered.

" I'm going to have the little carriage, and Baptiste can drive,—so you'll have nothing to do but keep your gloves nice," returned Amy, with a glance at the immaculate kids, which were a weak point with Laurie.

" Then I'll go with pleasure," and he put out his hand for her sketch-book. But she tucked it under her arm with a sharp,—

" Don't trouble ; *you* don't look equal to it."

Laurie lifted his eyebrows, and followed at a leisurely pace as she ran down stairs ; but when they got into the carriage he took the reins himself, and left Baptiste to fall asleep on his perch.

The two never quarrelled ; Amy was too well-bred, and just now Laurie was too lazy ; so, in a minute he peeped under her hat-brim with an inquiring air ; she answered with a smile, and they went on together in the most amicable manner.

It was a lovely drive, along winding roads rich in the picturesque scenes that delight beauty-loving eyes. Here an ancient monastery, whence the solemn chanting of the monks came down to them. There a bare-legged shepherd, in wooden shoes, pointed hat, and rough jacket over one shoulder, sat piping on a stone, while his goats skipped among the rocks or lay at his feet. Gnarled olive-trees covered the hills with their dusky foliage, fruit hung golden in the orchard, and scarlet anemones fringed the roadside ; while beyond green slopes and craggy heights, the Maritime Alps rose against the blue Italian sky.

Valrosa well deserved its name—for roses covered the walls of the house, climbed the pillars, and ran riot over the balustrade of the wide terrace, whence one looked down on the sunny Mediterranean and the white-walled city on its shore.

" This is a regular honeymoon Paradise, isn't it ? Did you ever see such roses ! " asked Amy, pausing on the terrace to enjoy the view, and a whiff of perfume that came wandering by.

" No, nor felt such thorns," returned Laurie, with his thumb in his mouth, after a vain attempt to capture a solitary scarlet flower that grew just beyond his reach.

" Try lower down, and pick those that have no thorns," said Amy, deftly gathering three of the tiny cream-coloured ones that starred the wall behind her. She put them in his button-hole, as a peace-offering, and he stood a minute looking down at them with a curious expression, for he had thought of Jo in reaching after the thorny red rose. She had often worn ones like that, from the greenhouse at home. The pale roses Amy gave him were the sort that the Italians lay in dead hands—and, for a moment, he wondered if the omen was for Jo or for himself. But the next instant his American common sense got the better of sentimentality, and he laughed a heartier laugh than Amy had heard since he came.

" It's good advice—you'd better take it and save your fingers," she said, thinking her speech amused him.

" Thank you, I will ! " he answered in jest—and a few months later he did it in earnest.

" Laurie, when are you going to your grandfather ? " she asked, presently, as she settled herself on a rustic seat.

" Very soon."

"He expects you, and you really ought to go."

"Hospitable creature ! I know it."

"Then why don't you do it ? "

"Natural depravity, I suppose."

"Natural indolence, you mean. It's really dreadful ! " and Amy looked severe.

"Not so bad as it seems, for I should only plague him if I went, so I might as well stay, and plague you a little longer—you can bear it better ; in fact, I think it agrees with you excellently ! " and Laurie composed himself for a lounge on the broad ledge of the balustrade.

"What would Jo say if she saw you now ? " asked Amy impatiently, hoping to stir him up by the mention of her energetic sister's name.

"As usual : ' Go away, Teddy, I'm busy ! ' " He laughed as he spoke, but a shade passed over his face, for the utterance of the familiar name touched the wound that was not healed yet. Both tone and shadow struck Amy, for she looked up in time to catch a new expression on Laurie's face—a hard, bitter look, full of pain, dissatisfaction, and regret. It was gone before she could study it, and the listless expression back again.

Laurie saw and understood the affectionate anxiety which she hesitated to express, and looking straight into her eyes, said, just as he used to say to her mother,—

"It's all right, ma'am ! "

That satisfied her, and set at rest the doubts that had begun to worry her lately. It also touched her, and she showed that it did, by the cordial tone in which she said,—

"I'm glad of that ! I fancied you might have wasted money at that wicked Baden-Baden, or got into some of the scrapes that young men seem to consider a necessary part of a foreign tour. Don't stay out there in the sun, come and lie on the grass here, and ' let us be friendly,' as Jo used to say when we got in the sofa-corner and told secrets."

Laurie obediently threw himself down on the turf, and began to amuse himself by sticking daisies into the ribbons of Amy's hat, that lay there.

"When do you begin your great work of art, Raphaella ? " he asked, changing the subject abruptly after another pause, in which he had been wondering if Amy knew his secret, and wanted to talk about it.

" Never ! " she answered, with a decided air. " Rome took all the vanity out of me, for after seeing the wonders there, I gave up all my foolish hopes in despair."

" Why should you, with so much energy and talent ? "

" That's just why, because talent isn't genius, and no amount of energy can make it so. I won't be a common-place dauber, so I don't intend to try any more."

" And what are you going to do with yourself now, if I may ask ? "

" Polish up my other talents, and be an ornament to society, if I get the chance."

It was a characteristic speech, and sounded daring; but audacity becomes young people, and Amy's ambition had a good foundation. Laurie smiled, but he liked the spirit with which she took up a new purpose, when a long cherished one had died, and spent no time lamenting.

" Good ! and here is where Fred Vaughn comes in, I fancy."

Amy preserved a discreet silence, but there was a conscious look in her downcast face, that made Laurie sit up and say gravely,—

" You are not engaged, I hope ? " and Laurie looked very elder-brotherly and grave all of a sudden.

" No."

" But you will be, if he comes back and goes properly down upon his knees, won't you ? "

" Very likely."

" Then you are fond of old Fred ? "

" I could be if I tried."

" But you don't intend to try till the proper moment ? Bless my soul, what unearthly prudence ! He's a good fellow, Amy, but not the man I fancied you'd like."

" He is rich, a gentleman, and has delightful manners," —began Amy trying to be quite cool and dignified, but feeling a little ashamed of herself, in spite of the sincerity of her intentions.

Laurie laid himself down again, with a sense of disappointment which he could not explain. His look and silence, as well as a certain inward self-disapproval, ruffled Amy—and made her resolve to deliver her lecture without delay.

" I wish you'd do me the favour to rouse yourself a little," she said sharply.

" Do it for me, there's a dear girl ! "

" I could if I tried," and she looked as if she would like doing it in the most summary style.

" Try, then, I give you leave," returned Laurie, who enjoyed having some one to tease, after his long abstinence from his favourite pastime.

" Flo and I have got a new name for you ; it's ' Lazy Laurence ; ' how do you like it ? "

She thought it would annoy him, but he only folded his arms, with an imperturbable—" That's not bad ! thank you, ladies."

" Do you want to know what I honestly think of you ? "

" Pining to be told ? "

" Well, I despise you."

" Why, if you please ? "

" Because with every chance for being good, useful, and happy, you are faulty, lazy, and miserable."

"Isn't a fellow to have any pleasure after a four-years' grind ? "

" You don't look as if you'd had much ; at any rate you are none the better for it, as far as I can see. I said when we first met, that you had improved ; now I take it all back, for I don't think you half so nice as when I left you at home. With money, talent, position, health, and beauty—ah, you like that, old vanity ! but it's the truth, so I can't help saying it—with all these splendid things to use and enjoy, you can find nothing to do but dawdle, and instead of being the man you might and ought to be, you are only—" there she stopped, with a look that had both pain and pity in it.

In a minute a hand came down over the page, so that she could not draw, and Laurie's voice said, with a droll imitation of a penitent child,—

" I will be good ! oh, I will be good ! "

But Amy did not laugh, for she was in earnest ; and, tapping on the outspread hand with her pencil, said soberly,—

" Aren't you ashamed of a hand like that ? It's as soft and white as a woman's, and looks as if it never did any-thing but wear Jouvin's best gloves, and pick flowers for ladies. You are not a dandy, thank heaven ! so I'm glad to see there are no diamonds or big seal rings on it, only

the little old one Jo gave you so long ago. Dear soul!
I wish she was here to help me."

"So do I!"

The hand vanished as suddenly as it came, and there
was energy enough in the echo of her wish to suit even
Amy. She glanced down at him with a new thought in
her mind—but he was lying with his hat half over his
face, as if for shade, and his moustache hid his mouth.
She remembered that Laurie never spoke voluntarily of
Jo; she recalled the shadow on his face just now, the
change in his character, and the wearing of the little old
ring, which was no ornament to a handsome hand. Amy
had fancied that perhaps a love-trouble was at the bottom
of the alteration, and now she was sure of it; her eyes
filled, and she spoke again, in a voice beautifully soft and
kind.

" I know I have no right to talk so to you, Laurie; and
if you weren't the sweetest-tempered fellow in the world,
you'd be very angry with me. But we are all so fond and
proud of you, I couldn't bear to think they should be
disappointed in you at home as I have been—though
perhaps they would understand the change better than
I do."

" I think they would," came from under the hat, in a
grim tone, quite as touching as a broken one.

" They ought to have told me, and not let me go
blundering and scolding, when I should have been more
kind and patient than ever. I never did like that Miss
Randal, and now I hate her!" said artful Amy—wishing
to be sure of her facts.

" Hang Miss Randal!" said Laurie, with a look that
left no doubt of his sentiments toward that young lady.

" I beg pardon; I thought—" she paused diplo-
matically.

" No, you didn't; you knew perfectly well I never cared
for anyone but Jo," Laurie said that in his old, impetuous
tone, and turned his face away as he spoke.

" I did think so; but as they never said anything about
it, and you came away, I supposed I was mistaken. And
Jo wouldn't be kind to you? Why, I was sure she loved
you dearly."

" She *was* kind, but not in the right way; and it's lucky
for her she didn't love me, if I'm the good-for-nothing

fellow you think me.   Do you think Jo would despise me
as you do ? "

"Yes, if she saw you now.   She hates lazy people.
Why don't you do something splendid, and *make* her
love you ? "

"I did my best, but it was no use."

"Graduating well, you mean.   That was no more than
you ought to have done, for your grandfather's sake.   It
would have been shameful to fail after spending so much
time and money, when everyone knew you *could* do well."

Neither spoke for several minutes.   Laurie sat turning
the little ring on his finger, and Amy put the last touches
to the hasty sketch she had been working at while she
talked.   Presently she put it on his knee, merely saying,—

"How do you like that ? "

He looked and then he smiled—as he could not well help
doing, for it was capitally done.   The long, lazy figure on
the grass, with listless face, half-shut eyes, and one hand
holding a cigar, from which came the little wreath of
smoke that encircled the dreamer's head.

"How well you draw ! " he said, with genuine surprise
and pleasure at her skill, adding, with a half laugh, "Yes,
that's me."

"As you are—this is as you were," and Amy laid
another sketch beside the one he held.

It was not nearly so well done, but there was a life and
spirit in it which atoned for many faults, and it recalled
the past so vividly that a sudden change swept over the
young man's face as he looked.   Only a rough sketch of
Laurie taming a horse ; hat and coat were off, and every
line of the active figure, resolute face, and commanding
attitude, was full of energy and meaning.   Laurie said
nothing ; but, as his eye went from one to the other, Amy
saw him flush up and fold his lips together as if he read
and accepted the little lesson she had given him.

"Much obliged !   You've improved immensely since
then, and I congratulate you.   May I venture to suggest
in ' a honeymoon Paradise,' that five o'clock is the dinner
hour at your hotel ? "

Laurie rose as he spoke, returned the pictures with a
smile and a bow, and looked at his watch, as if to remind
her that even moral lectures should have an end.   He
tried to resume his former easy, indifferent air, but it *was*

an affectation now—for the rousing had been more efficacious than he would confess. Amy felt the shade of coldness in his manner, and said to herself,—

"Now I've offended him. Well, if it does him good, I'm glad—if it makes him hate me, I'm sorry ; but it's true, and I can't take back a word of it."

Next morning, instead of the usual call, Amy received a note which made her smile at the beginning, and sigh at the end :—

"MY DEAR MENTOR,—

"Please make my adieux to your aunt, and exult within yourself for 'Lazy Laurence' has gone to his grandpa, like the best of boys. A pleasant winter to you, and may the gods grant you a blissful honeymoon at Valrosa. I think Fred would be benefited by a rouser. Tell him so, with my congratulations.

"Yours gratefully,
"TELEMACHUS."

"Good boy ! I'm glad he's gone," said Amy, with an approving smile ; adding, with an involuntary sigh,—
"But how I shall miss him."

CHAPTER XVII

THE VALLEY OF THE SHADOW

WHEN the first bitterness was over, the family accepted the inevitable, and tried to bear it cheerfully. The pleasantest room in the house was set apart for Beth, and in it was gathered everything that she most loved—flowers, pictures, her piano, the little work-table, and the beloved pussies. Father's best books found their way there, mother's easy chair, Jo's desk, Amy's loveliest sketches ; and every day Meg brought her babies on a loving pilgrimage, to make sunshine for Aunty Beth.

John quietly set apart a little sum, that he might enjoy
the pleasure of keeping the invalid supplied with the fruit
she loved and longed for ; old Hannah never wearied of
concocting dainty dishes to tempt a capricious appetite,
dropping tears as she worked ; and, from across the sea,
came little gifts and cheerful letters, seeming to bring
breaths of warmth and fragrance from lands that know
no winter.

Here, cherished like a household saint in a shrine, sat
Beth, tranquil and busy as ever ; for nothing could change
the sweet, unselfish nature ; and even while preparing to
leave life, she tried to make it happier for those who
should remain behind. The feeble fingers were never idle,
and one of her pleasures was to make little things for the
school-children daily passing to and fro. To drop a pair
of mittens from her window for a pair of purple hands, a
needle-book for some small mother of many dolls, pen-
wipers for young penmen toiling through forests of pot-
hooks, scrap-books for picture-loving eyes, and all manner
of pleasant devices, till the reluctant climbers up the ladder
of learning came to regard the gentle giver as a sort of
fairy godmother, who showered down gifts miraculously
suited to their tastes and needs. If Beth wanted any
reward, she found it in the bright little faces always turned
up to her window, with nods and smiles, and the droll
little letters which came to her, full of blots and gratitude.

It was well for all that this peaceful time was given them
as preparation for the sad hours to come ; for, by-and-by,
Beth said the needle was " so heavy," and put it down
for ever ; talking wearied her, faces troubled her, pain
claimed her for its own, and her tranquil spirit was sorrowfully perturbed by the ills that vexed her feeble flesh.

Jo never left her for an hour since Beth had said, " I feel
stronger when you are here." She slept on a couch in
the room, waking often to renew the fire, to feed, lift, or
wait upon the patient creature who seldom asked for
anything, and " tried not to be a trouble." All day she
haunted the room, jealous of any other nurse, and prouder
of being chosen then than of any honour her life had ever
brought her.

One night, when Beth looked among the books upon her
table, to find something to make her forget the mortal
weariness that was almost as hard to bear as pain, as she

turned the leaves of her old favourite *Pilgrim's Progress*,
she found a little paper scribbled over, in Jo's hand.
The name caught her eye, and the blurred lines made her
sure that tears had fallen on it.

"Poor Jo, she's fast asleep, so I won't wake her to ask
leave ; she shows me all her things, and I don't think
she'll mind if I look at this," thought Beth, with a glance
at her sister, who lay on the rug, with the tongs beside her,
ready to wake up the minute the log fell apart.

"MY BETH.

"Sitting patient in the shadow
    Till the blessed light shall come,
A serene and saintly presence
    Sanctifies our troubled home.
Earthly joys, and hopes, and sorrows,
    Break like ripples on the strand
Of the deep and silent river
    Where her willing feet now stand.

"Oh, my sister, passing from me,
    Out of human care and strife,
Leave me as a gift, those virtues
    Which have beautified your life.
Dear, bequeath me that great patience
    Which has power to sustain
A cheerful, uncomplaining spirit
    In its prison-house of pain.

"Give me, for I need it sorely,
    Of that courage, wise and sweet,
Which has made the path of duty
    Green beneath your willing feet.
Give me that unselfish nature,
    That with charity divine,
Can pardon wrong for love's dear sake —
    Meek heart forgive me mine !

"Thus our parting daily loseth
    Something of its bitter pain,
And while learning this hard lesson,
    My great loss becomes my gain.

> For the touch of grief will render
>   My wild nature more serene,
> Give to life new aspirations—
>   A new trust in the unseen.
>
> " Henceforth, safe across the river,
>   I shall see for evermore
> A beloved, household spirit
>   Waiting for me on the shore.
> Hope and faith, born of my sorrow,
>   Guardian angels shall become,
> And the sister gone before me,
>   By their hands shall lead me home."

Blurred and blotted, faulty and feeble, as the lines were, they brought a look of inexpressible comfort to Beth's face, for her one regret had been that she had done so little ; and this seemed to assure her that her life had not been uesless—that her death would not bring the despair she feared. As she sat with the paper folded between her hands, the charred log fell asunder. Jo started up, revived the blaze, and crept to the bedside, hoping Beth slept.

" Not asleep, but so happy, dear. See, I found this, and read it ; I knew you wouldn't care. Have I been all that to you, Jo ? " she asked, with wistful, humble earnestness.

" Oh, Beth, so much, so much ! " and Jo's head went down upon the pillow, beside her sister's.

" Then I don't feel as if I'd wasted my life. I'm not so good as you make me, but I *have* tried to do right ; and now, when it's too late to begin even to do better, it's such a comfort to know that someone loves me so much, and feels as if I'd helped her."

" More than anyone in the world, Beth. I used to think I couldn't let you go ; but I'm learning to feel that even death can't part us, though it seems to."

" I know it cannot, and I don't fear it any longer, for I'm sure I shall be your Beth still, to love and help you more than ever. You must take my place, Jo, and be everything to father and mother when I'm gone."

" I'll try, Beth ; " and then and there Jo renounced her old ambition, and pledged herself to a new and better one.

As Beth had hoped, the " tide went out easily ; " and in the dark hour before the dawn, on the bosom where she

Jo was alone in the twilight, lying on the old sofa, looking
at the fire and thinking.

[*see page 124*

had drawn her first breath, she quietly drew her last, with no farewell but one loving look and a little sigh.

When morning came, for the first time in many months the fire was out, Jo's place was empty, and the room was very still. But the spring sunshine streamed in like a bene-diction, upon a face so full of painless peace, that those who loved it best smiled through their tears, and thanked God that Beth was well at last.

CHAPTER XVIII

LEARNING TO FORGET

AMY'S lecture did Laurie good, though, of course, he did not own it till long afterward. Laurie went back to his grandfather, and was so dutifully devoted for several weeks that the old gentleman declared the climate of Nice had improved him wonderfully, and he had better try it again. There was nothing the young gentleman would have liked better—but whenever the longing grew very strong, he fortified his resolution by repeating the words that had made the deepest impression—" I despise you ; "   " Go and do something splendid that will *make* her love you."

Laurie turned the matter over in his mind so often that he soon brought himself to confess that he *had* been selfish and lazy. Jo *wouldn't* love him, but he might *make* her respect and admire him by doing something which should prove that a girl's " No " had not spoilt his life. He had always meant to do something, and so Laurie resolved to embalm his love-sorrow in music, and compose a Requiem which should harrow up Jo's soul and melt the heart of every hearer. So the next time the old gentleman found him getting restless and moody, and ordered him off, he went to Vienna, where he had musical friends, and fell to work with the firm determination to distinguish himself. But, whether the sorrow was too vast to be embodied in music, or music too ethereal to uplift a mortal woe, he soon discovered that the Requiem was beyond

H

him, just at present. It was evident that his mind was
not in working order yet, and his ideas needed clarifying ;
for often, in the middle of a plaintive strain, he would find
himself humming a dancing tune that vividly recalled the
Christmas ball at Nice—especially the stout Frenchman—
and put an effectual stop to tragic composition for the
time being. He finally came to the wise conclusion that
everyone who loved music was not a composer. Returning
from one of Mozart's grand Operas, splendidly performed at
the Royal Theatre, he looked over his own, played a few of
the best parts, sat staring up at the busts of Mendelssohn,
Beethoven, and Bach, who stared benignly back again ;
then suddenly he tore up his music sheets, one by one,
and, as the last fluttered out of his hand, he said soberly,
to himself—

"She is right ! talent isn't genius. That music has
taken the vanity out of me as Rome took it out of her,
and I won't be a humbug any longer. Now what shall
I do ? "

That seemed a hard question to answer, and Laurie
began to wish he had to work for his daily bread. He had
thought that the task of forgetting his love for Jo would
absorb all his powers for years ; but, to his great surprise,
he discovered it grew easier every day. He refused to
believe it at first—got angry with himself, and couldn't
understand it ; but these hearts of ours are curious and
contrary things, and time and nature work their will in
spite of us. Laurie's heart *wouldn't* ache ; the wound
persisted in healing with a rapidity that astonished him,
and, instead of trying to forget, he found himself trying to
remember. He had not foreseen this turn of affairs, and
was not prepared for it. He carefully stirred up the
embers of his lost love, but they refused to burst into a
blaze, and he was reluctantly obliged to confess that the
boyish passion was slowly subsiding into a brotherly
affection which would last unbroken to the end.

As the word "brotherly" passed through his mind in
one of these reveries, he smiled, and glanced up at the
picture of Mozart that was before him——

"Well, he was a great man ; and when he couldn't have
one sister he took the other, and was happy," he thought,
and the next instant kissed the little old ring, saying to
himself—

" No, I won't! I haven't forgotten; I never can. I'll try again, and if that fails, why then——"

Leaving his sentence unfinished, he seized pen and paper and wrote to Jo, telling her that he could not settle to anything while there was the least hope of her changing her mind. Couldn't she, wouldn't she—and let him come home and be happy? While waiting for an answer he did nothing—but he did it energetically, for he was in a fever of impatience. It came at last, and settled his mind effectually on one point—for Jo begged him to be happy with somebody else, but always to keep a little corner of his heart for his loving sister Jo. In a postscript she desired him not to tell Amy that Beth was worse; but write to her often, and not let her feel lonely, homesick, or anxious.

" So I will, at once. Poor little girl; it will be a sad going home for her, I'm afraid; " and Laurie opened his desk, as if writing to Amy had been the proper conclusion of the sentence left unfinished some weeks before.

The letter went very soon, and was promptly answered, for Amy *was* homesick, and confessed it in the most delightfully confiding manner. Laurie went back to Paris, hoping somebody would arrive before long. He wanted desperately to go to Nice, but would not till he was asked; and Amy would not ask him, for just then she was having experiences of her own, which made her rather wish to avoid the quizzical eyes of " our boy."

Fred Vaughn had returned, and put the question to which she had once decided to answer " Yes, thank you; " but now she said, " No, thank you," kindly but steadily; the words " Fred is a good fellow, but not at all the man I fancied you would ever like," and Laurie's face, when he uttered them, kept returning to her as pertinaciously as her own did, when she said in look, if not in words, " I shall marry for money." It troubled her to remember that; now she wished she could take it back, it sounded so unwomanly.

She grew a little pale and pensive that spring, and went out sketching alone a good deal. She never had much to show when she came home, but she sat for hours with her hands folded, on the terrace at Valrosa, or absently sketched any fancy that occurred to her. Her aunt thought that she regretted her answer to Fred; and, finding denials

useless, Amy left her to think what she liked, taking care
that Laurie should know that Fred had gone to Egypt.
That was all, but he understood it, and looked relieved,
as he said to himself, with a venerable air,—

"I was sure she would think better of it. Poor old
fellow, I've been through it all, and I can sympathize."

With that he heaved a great sigh, put his feet up on the
sofa, and enjoyed Amy's letter luxuriously.

While these changes were going on abroad, trouble had
come at home; but the letter telling that Beth was failing,
never reached Amy; and when the next found her, the
grass was green above her sister. The sad news met her
at Vevey, for they had travelled slowly to Switzerland, by
way of Genoa and the Italian lakes. She quietly submitted to the family decree, that she should not shorten
her visit, since it was too late to say good-bye to Beth, but
she longed to be at home; and every day looked wistfully
across the lake, waiting for Laurie to come and comfort
her.

He did come very soon; for the same mail brought
letters to them both, but he was in Germany, and it took
some days to reach him. The moment he read it, he
packed his knapsack, and was off to keep his promise,
with a heart full of joy and sorrow, hope and suspense.

He knew Vevey well; and as soon as the boat touched
the little quay, he hurried along the shore to La Tour,
where the Carrols were living *en pension*. The garçon was
in despair that the whole family had gone to take a
promenade—but no, the blonde mademoiselle might be in
the château garden. At one corner of the pleasant old
garden, was a seat, and here Amy often came to console
herself with the beauty all about her. She was sitting
here that day, leaning her head on her hand, with a homesick heart and heavy eyes, thinking of Beth, and wondering
why Laurie did not come. She did not hear him cross the
court-yard beyond, nor see him pause in the archway that
led into the garden. He stood a minute, looking at her
with new eyes, seeing what no one had ever seen before—
the tender side of Amy's character. Everything about
her mutely suggested love and sorrow; the blotted letters
in her lap, the black ribbon that tied up her hair, the
womanly pain and patience in her face; even the little
ebony cross at her throat seemed pathetic to Laurie, for

he had given it to her, and she wore it as her only ornament.
If he had any doubts about the reception she would give
him, they were set at rest the minute she looked up and
saw him ; for, dropping everything, she ran to him,
exclaiming in a tone of unmistakable love and longing,—

"Oh, Laurie, Laurie ! I knew you'd come to me ! "

I think everything was said and settled then ; for, as
they stood together quite silent for a moment, with the
dark head bent down protectingly over the light one, Amy
felt that no one could comfort and sustain her so well as
Laurie, and Laurie decided that Amy was the only woman
in the world who could fill Jo's place, and make him
happy. He did not tell her so ; but both felt the truth,
were satisfied, and gladly left the rest to silence.

"It was such a surprise to look up and find you, just as
I was beginning to fear you wouldn't come," she said at
last, trying to speak naturally.

"I came the minute I heard. I wish I could say something to comfort you for the loss of dear little Beth, but
I can only feel, and—" he could not get any further, for
he, too, turned bashful all of a sudden, and did not quite
know what to say. So he took her hand, and gave it a
sympathetic squeeze that was better than words.

"You needn't say anything,—this comforts me," she
said, softly. "Beth is well and happy, and I mustn't
wish her back,—but I dread the going home, much as
I long to see them all. We won't talk about it now, for
I want to enjoy you while you stay. You needn't go
right back, need you ? "

"Not if you want me, dear."

"I do, so much ! Aunt and Flo are very kind, but you
seem like one of the family, and it would be so comfortable
to have you for a little while."

Amy spoke and looked so like a homesick child whose
heart was full, that Laurie forgot his bashfulness all at
once, and gave her just what she wanted,—the petting
she was used to, and the cheerful conversation she needed.

The moment Mrs. Carrol saw the girl's altered face she
was illuminated with a new idea, and exclaimed to herself,
"Now I understand it all,—the child has been pining for
young Laurence. Bless my heart ! I never thought of
such a thing ! "

With praiseworthy discretion, the good lady said

nothing, but cordially urged Laurie to stay, and begged
Amy to enjoy his society, for it would do her more good
than so much solitude. Amy was a model of docility;
and, as her aunt was a good deal occupied with Flo, she
was left to entertain her friend, and did it with more than
her usual success.

The invigorating air did them both good, and much
exercise worked wholesome changes in minds as well as
bodies. In spite of the new sorrow it was a very happy
time,—so happy that Laurie could not bear to disturb it
by a word. It took him a little while to recover from his
surprise at the rapid cure of his first, and, as he had firmly
believed, his only love. His first wooing had been of the
tempestuous order, and he looked back upon it as if
through a vista of years with a feeling of compassion
blended with regret. His second wooing he resolved
should be as calm and simple as possible; there was
hardly any need of telling Amy that he loved her; she
knew it without words, and had given him his answer
long ago. It all came about so naturally that no one
could complain, and he knew that everybody would be
pleased,—even Jo.

They had been floating about one morning, from gloomy
St. Gingolf to sunny Montreux, with pretty Vevey in the
valley, and Lausanne upon the hill beyond, a cloudless
blue sky overhead, and the bluer lake below. Amy had
been dabbling her hand in the water, and, when she looked
up, Laurie was leaning on his oars, with an expression in
his eyes that made her say, hastily—merely for the sake
of saying something—

"You must be tired,—let me row; it will do me good,
for since you came I have been altogether lazy and
luxurious."

"I'm not tired, but you may take an oar if you like.
There's room enough, though I have to sit nearly in the
middle, else the boat won't trim," returned Laurie, as if he
rather liked the arrangement.

Feeling that she had not mended matters much, Amy
took the offered third of a seat, and accepted an oar.
She rowed as well as she did many other things; the boat
went smoothly through the water.

"How well we pull together, don't we?" said Amy,
who objected to silence just then.

"So well, that I wish we might always pull in the same boat. Will you, Amy?" very tenderly.

"Yes, Laurie!" very low.

Then they both stopped rowing, and added a pretty little *tableau* of human love and happiness to the dissolving views reflected in the lake.

CHAPTER XIX

ALL ALONE

IT was easy to promise self-abegnation when self was wrapt up in another, and heart and soul were purified by a sweet example; but when the helpful voice was silent, the beloved presence gone, and nothing remained but loneliness and grief, then Jo found her promise very hard to keep. How could she "comfort father and mother," when her own heart ached with a ceaseless longing for her sister; how could she "make the house cheerful," when all its light, and warmth, and beauty seemed to have deserted it when Beth left the old home for the new? Poor Jo! these were dark days to her, for something like despair came over her when she thought of spending all her life in that quiet house, devoted to humdrum cares, a few poor little pleasures, and the duty that never seemed to grow any easier. "I can't do it. I shall break away and do something desperate if somebody doesn't come and help me," she said to herself, when her first efforts failed, and she fell into the miserable state of mind which comes when strong wills have to yield to the inevitable. Often she started up at night, thinking Beth called her; and when the sight of the little empty bed made her cry with the bitter cry of an unsubmissive sorrow. "Oh, Beth! come back! come back!" she did not stretch out her yearning arms in vain; for, as quick to hear her sobbing as she had been to hear her sister's faintest whisper, her mother came to comfort her.

Sacred moments! when heart talked to heart, in the silence of the night, turning affliction to a blessing, which chastened grief, and strengthened love. Feeling this, Jo's burden seemed easier to bear, and her troubled mind likewise found help; for one day she went to the study, and leaning over the good grey head lifted to welcome her with a tranquil smile, she said, very humbly,

"Father, talk to me as you did to Beth. I need it more than she did, for I'm all wrong."

"My dear, nothing can comfort me like this," he answered, with a falter in his voice, and both arms round her, as if he, too, needed help, and did not fear to ask it.

Other helps had Jo, humble duties, that would not be denied their part in serving her, and which she slowly learned to see and value. Brooms and dishcloths never could be so distasteful as they once had been, for Beth had presided over both; and something of her housewifely spirit seemed to linger round the little mop and the old brush, that was never thrown away. As she used them, Jo found herself humming the songs Beth used to hum, imitating Beth's orderly ways, and giving the little touches here and there that kept everything fresh and cozy, which was the first step toward making the home happy, though she didn't know it, till Hannah said, with an approving squeeze of the hand,—

"You thoughtful creter, you're determined we shan't miss that dear lamb, ef you can help it. We don't say much, but we see it, and the Lord will bless you for't, see ef He don't."

As they sat sewing together, Jo discovered how much improved her sister Meg was; how well she could talk, how happy she was in husband and children, and how much they were all doing for each other.

"Marriage is an excellent thing after all. I wonder if I should blossom out, half as well as you have, if I tried it, always 'perwisin' I could," said Jo, as she constructed a kite for Demi, in the topsy-turvy nursery.

"It's just what you need to bring out the womanly half of your nature, Jo. You are like a chestnut burr, prickly outside, but silky-soft within, and a sweet kernel, if one can only get at it. Love will make you show your heart some day, and then the rough burr will fall off."

"Frost opens chestnut burrs, ma'am, and it takes a good shake to bring them down. Boys go nutting, and I don't care to be bagged by them," returned Jo, pasting away at the kite, which no wind that blows would ever carry up, for Daisy had tied herself on as a bob.

Meg laughed, for she was glad to see a glimmer of Jo's old spirit, but she felt it her duty to enforce her opinion by every argument in her power; and the sisterly chats were not wasted, especially as two of Meg's most effective arguments were the babies, whom Jo loved tenderly.

"Why don't you write? that always used to make you happy," said her mother once, when the desponding fit overshadowed Jo.

"I've no heart to write, and if I had, nobody cares for my things."

"We do; write something for us, and never mind the rest of the world. Try it, dear; I'm sure it would do you good, and please us very much."

"Don't believe I can;" but Jo got out her desk, and began to overhaul her half-finished manuscripts.

An hour afterward her mother peeped in, and there she was scratching away, with her black pinafore on, and an absorbed expression, which caused Mrs. March to smile, and slip away, well pleased with the result of her suggestion. Jo never knew how it happened, but something got into that story that went straight to the hearts of those who read it; for, when her family had laughed and cried over it, her father sent it, much against her will to one of the popular magazines, and, to her utter surprise, it was not only paid for, but others requested. Letters from several persons, whose praise was honour, followed the appearance of the little story, newspapers copied it, and strangers as well as friends admired it. For a small thing, it was a great success; and Jo was more astonished than when her novel was commended and condemned all at once.

"I don't understand it; what *can* there be in a simple little story like that, to make people praise it so?" she said, quite bewildered.

"There is truth in it, Jo—that's the secret! humour and pathos make it alive, and you have found your style at last. You wrote with no thought of fame or money, and put your heart into it, my daughter; you have had the bitter, now comes the sweet; do your best, and grow as happy as we are in your success.''

"If there *is* anything good or true in what I write, it isn't mine; I owe it all to you and mother, and to Beth," said Jo, more touched by her father's words than by any amount of praise from the world.

When Amy and Laurie wrote of their engagement, Mrs. March feared that Jo would find it difficult to rejoice over it, but her fears were soon set at rest.

"You like it, mother?" said Jo, as they laid down the closely written sheets, and looked at one another.

"Yes, I hoped it would be so, ever since Amy wrote that she had refused Fred. I felt sure then that something better than what you call 'the mercenary spirit' had come over her, and a hint here and there in her letters made me suspect that love and Laurie would win the day."

"How sharp you are, Marmee, and how silent; you never said a word to me."

"Mothers have need of sharp eyes and discreet tongues, when they have girls to manage. I was half afraid to put the idea into your head, lest you should write and congratulate them before the thing was settled."

"I'm not the scatter-brain I was; you may trust me, I'm sober and sensible enough for anyone's *confidante* now."

"So you are, dear, and I should have made you mine, only I fancied it might have pained you to learn that your Teddy loved anyone else."

"Now, mother, did you really think I could be so silly and selfish, after I'd refused his love, when it was freshest, if not best?"

"I knew you were sincere then, Jo, but lately I have thought that if he came back, and asked again, you might, perhaps, feel like giving another answer."

"No, mother, it is better as it is, and I'm glad Amy has learned to love him. But you are right in one thing; I am lonely, and perhaps if Teddy had tried again, I might have said 'Yes,' not because I love him any more, but because I care more to be loved, than when he went away."

"I'm glad of that, Jo, for it shows that you are getting on. There are plenty to love you, so try to be satisfied with father and mother, sisters and brothers, friends and babies, till the best lover of all comes to give you your reward."

" Mothers are the *best* lovers in the world ; but I don't mind whispering to Marmee, that I'd like to try all kinds. It's very curious, but the more I try to satisfy myself with all sorts of natural affections, the more I seem to want.   I'd no idea hearts could take in so many—mine is elastic, it never seems full now, and I used to be quite contented with my family ; I don't understand it."

" I do," and Mrs. March smiled her wise smile, as Jo turned back the leaves and read what Amy said of Laurie.

By-and-by, Jo roamed away upstairs, for it was rainy, and she could not walk. Up in the garret, where Jo's unquiet wanderings ended, stood four little wooden chests in a row, each marked with its owner's name, and each filled with relics of the childhood and girlhood ended now for all. Jo glanced into them, and when she came to her own stared absently at a bundle of old exercise-books which caught her eye. She turned them over, and re-lived that pleasant winter at kind Mrs. Kirke's. She had smiled at first, then she looked thoughtful, next sad, and when she came to a little message written in the Professor's hand, her lips began to tremble, the books slid out of her lap, and she sat looking at the friendly words, as if they took a new meaning, and touched a tender spot in her heart.

" Wait for me, my friend, I may be a little late, but I shall surely come."

" Oh, if he only would ! So kind, so good, so patient with me always ; my dear old Fritz, I didn't value him half enough when I had him, but now how I should love to see him, for everyone seems going away from me, and I'm all alone."

And holding the little paper fast, as if it were a promise yet to be fulfilled, Jo laid her head down on a ragbag and cried, as if in opposition to the rain pattering on the roof.

Was it all loneliness, or was it the awakening of a sentiment which had bided its time as patiently as its inspirer ? Who shall say ?

CHAPTER XX

SURPRISES

Jo was alone in the twilight, lying on the old sofa, looking at the fire and thinking. It was her favourite way of spending the hour of dusk; and she used to lie there, planning stories, dreaming dreams, or thinking tender thoughts of the sister who never seemed far away. Her face looked tired and rather sad; for to-morrow was her birthday, and she was thinking how fast the years went by, and how little she seemed to have accomplished. Almost twenty-five, and nothing to show for it. She thought, adding—

"An old maid—that's what I'm to be. A literary spinster, with a pen for a spouse, a family of stories for children, and twenty years hence a morsel of fame, perhaps. Well, I dare say, old maids are very comfortable when they get used to it; but—— " and there Jo sighed, as if the prospect was not inviting.

It seldom is, and thirty seems the end of all things to five-and-twenty; but it's not so bad as it looks, and one can get on quite happily if one has something in one's self to fall back upon.

Jo must have fallen asleep for, suddenly, Laurie's ghost seemed to stand before her. Like Jenny in the ballad—

> "She could not think it he,"

and lay staring up at him, in startled silence, till he stooped and kissed her. Then she flew up, crying joyfully—

"Oh my Teddy! Oh my Teddy!"

"Dear Jo, you are glad to see me, then?"

"Glad! my blessed boy, words can't express my gladness. Where's Amy?"

"Your mother has got her down at Meg's. We stopped there by the way, and there was no getting my wife out of their clutches."

" Your what ? " cried Jo—for Laurie uttered those two words with an unconscious pride which betrayed him.

" Oh, the dickens ! now I've done it " ; and he looked so guilty that Jo was down on him like a flash.

" You've gone and got married ? "

" Yes, please, but I never will again " ; and he went down upon his knees with a penitent clasping of hands, and a face full of mischief, mirth, and triumph.

" Mercy on us ; what dreadful thing will you do next ? " and Jo fell into her seat with a gasp.

" A characteristic, but not exactly complimentary congratulation," returned Laurie, still in an abject attitude, but beaming with satisfaction.

" What can you expect, when you take one's breath away, creeping in like a burglar, and letting cats out of bags like that ? Get up, you ridiculous boy, and tell me all about it."

" Not a word, unless you let me come in my old place, and promise not to barricade."

Jo laughed as she had not done for many a long day, and patted the sofa invitingly, as she said in a cordial tone—

" The old pillow is up garret, and we don't need it now ; so, come and 'fess, Teddy."

" How good it sounds to hear you say ' Teddy ' ; no one ever calls me that but you " ; and Laurie sat down with an air of great content.

" What does Amy call you ? "

" My lord."

" That's like her—well, you look it " ; and Jo's eyes plainly betrayed that she found her boy comelier than ever.

The pillow was gone, but there *was* a barricade, nevertheless ; a natural one raised by time, absence, and change of heart. It was gone directly, however, for Laurie said, with a vain attempt at dignity—

" Don't I look like a married man, and the head of a family ? "

" Not a bit, and you never will. You've grown bigger and bonnier, but you are the same scapegrace as ever."

" Now, really, Jo, you ought to treat me with more respect," began Laurie, who enjoyed it all immensely.

" How can I, when the mere idea of you, married and settled, is so irresistibly funny that I can't keep sober " answered Jo, smiling all over her face, so infectiously, that they had another laugh, and then settled down for a good talk, quite in the pleasant old fashion.

"It's no use your going out in the cold to get Amy, for they are all coming up, presently; I couldn't wait; I wanted to be the one to tell you the grand surprise."

"Of course you did, and spoilt your story by beginning at the wrong end. Now, start right, and tell me how it all happened; I'm pining to know."

"Well, I did it to please Amy," began Laurie, with a twinkle, that made Jo exclaim—

"Fib number one; Amy did it to please you. Go on, and tell the truth, if you can, sir."

"Now she's beginning to marm it, isn't it jolly to hear her?" said Laurie to the fire. "It's all the same, you know, she and I being one. We planned to come home with the Carrols but they decided to pass another winter in Paris. Grandpa wanted to come home; he went to please me, and I couldn't let him go alone, neither could I leave Amy; and Mrs. Carrol had got English notions about chaperons and wouldn't let Amy come with us. So I just settled the difficulty by saying, 'Let's be married, and then we can do as we like,'"

"Of course you did; you always have things to suit you."

"Not always"; and something in Laurie's voice made Jo say hastily—

"How did you ever get aunt to agree?"

"It was hard work; but, between us, we talked her over for we had heaps of good reasons on our side. There wasn't time to write and ask leave, and that charming arrangement would make everything easy all round; so we did it."

"When, where, how?" asked Jo, in a fever of feminine interest and curiosity, for she could not realize it a particle.

"Six weeks ago, at the American consul's, in Paris—a very quiet wedding, of course."

"Why didn't you let us know afterwards?" asked Jo, in a quieter tone, when they had sat quite still a minute.

"We wanted to surprise you; we thought we were coming directly home, at first, but the dear old gentleman, as soon as we were married, found he couldn't be ready under a month, at least, and sent us off to spend our honeymoon wherever we liked. Amy had once called Valrosa a regular honeymoon home, so we went there, and were as happy as people are but once in their lives."

Laurie seemed to forget Jo, for a minute, and she was glad of it ; for the fact that he had told her these things so freely and naturally, assured her that he had quite forgiven and forgotten. She tried to draw away her hand ; but, as if he guessed the thought that prompted the impulse, Laurie held it fast, and said gravely—

" Jo, dear, I want to say one thing, and then we'll put it by for ever. As I told you in my letter, when I wrote that Amy had been so kind to me, I shall never stop loving you ; but Amy and you change places in my heart, that's all. I could honestly share my heart between sister Jo and wife Amy, and love them both dearly. Will you believe it, and go back to the happy old times, when we first knew one another ? "

" I'll believe it, with all my heart ; but, Teddy, we never can be boy and girl again—the happy old times can't come back, and we mustn't expect it. We can't be playmates any longer, but we will be brother and sister, to love and help one another all our lives, won't we, Laurie ? "

He did not say a word, but took the hand she offered him, and laid his face down on it for a minute, feeling that out of the grave of a boyish passion, there had risen a beautiful, strong friendship to bless them both. Presently Jo said cheerfully, for she didn't want the coming home to be a sad one—

" I can't make it true that you children are really married, and going to set up housekeeping. Why, it seems only yesterday that I was buttoning Amy's pinafore, and pulling your hair when you teased. Mercy me, how time does fly ! "

" As one of the children is older than yourself, you needn't talk so like a grandma ; and when you see Amy, you will find her a rather precocious infant," said Laurie, looking amused at her maternal air.

" You may be a little older in years, but I'm ever so much older in feeling, Teddy. Women always are ; and this last year has been such a hard one, that I feel forty."

" Poor Jo ! we left you to bear it alone, while we went pleasuring. You've had a great deal to bear, and had to bear it all alone ; what a selfish beast I've been ! " and Laurie pulled his own hair, with a remorseful look.

But Jo answered in a tone which she tried to make quite cheerful—

"No, I had father and mother to help me, the dear babies to comfort me, and the thought that you and Amy were safe and happy, to make the troubles here easier to bear. I *am* lonely sometimes, but I daresay it's good for me, and—"

"You never shall be again," broke in Laurie; putting his arm about her, as if to fence out every human ill. "Amy and I can't get on without you, so you must come and teach the children to keep house."

"You always were a comfort, Teddy"; and Jo leaned her head on his shoulder, just as she did years ago, when Beth lay ill, and Laurie told her to hold on to him.

"You are the same Jo still, dropping tears about one minute, and laughing the next. You look a little wicked now; what is it, grandma?"

"I was wondering how you and Amy get on together."

"Like angels!"

"Yes, of course, at first—but which rules?"

"I don't mind telling you that she does, now; at least I let her think so—it pleases her, you know. By-and-by we shall take turns, for marriage, they say, halves one's rights and doubles one's duties."

"You'll go on as you begin, and Amy will rule you all the days of your life."

"Well, she does it so imperceptibly that I don't think I shall mind much. She winds one round her finger so softly and prettily as a skein of silk, and makes you feel as if she was doing you a favour all the while."

"That ever I should live to see you a henpecked husband and enjoying it!" cried Jo, with uplifted hands.

It was good to see Laurie square his shoulders, and smile with masculine scorn at that insinuation, as he replied, with his "high and mighty" air—

"Amy is too well-bred for that, and I am not the sort of man to submit to it. My wife and I respect one another too much ever to quarrel."

Jo liked that but the boy seemed changing very fast into the man, and regret mingled with her pleasure.

"I am sure of that; Amy and you never did quarrel as we used to. She is the sun, and I the wind in the fable, and the sun managed the man best, you remember."

" She can blow him up as well as shine on him," laughed Laurie. " Such a lecture as I got at Nice ! I give you my word it was a deal worse than any of your scoldings. A regular rouser."

" Well, if she abuses you, come to me, and I'll defend you ! "

" I look as if I needed it, don't I ? " said Laurie, getting up and striking an attitude which suddenly changed from the imposing to the rapturous, as Amy's voice was heard calling—

" Where is she ? where's my dear old Jo ? "

In trooped the whole family, and everyone was hugged and kissed and exulted over. Mr. Laurence, hale and hearty as ever, was quite as much improved as the others by his foreign tour, for the old-fashioned courtliness had received a polish which made it kindlier than ever. It was good to see him beam at " my children," as he called the young pair ; it was better still to see Amy pay him the daughterly duty and affection which completely won his old heart ; and, best of all, to watch Laurie revolve about the two as if never tired of enjoying the pretty picture they made.

Jo thought, as she watched the newly-weds, " How well they look together ! I was right, and Laurie has found the beautiful accomplished girl who will become his home better than clumsy old Jo, and be a pride, not a torment to him." Mrs. March and her husband smiled and nodded at each other with happy faces, for Amy's face was full of the soft brightness which betokens a peaceful heart, her voice had a new tenderness in it, both womanly and winning.

" Love has done much for our little girl," said her mother, softly.

" She has had a good example before her all her life, my dear," Mr. March whispered back, with a loving look at the worn face and grey head beside him.

Mercy on us, how they did talk ! first one, then the other, then all burst out together—trying to tell the history of three years in half an hour. It was fortunate that tea was at hand, to produce a lull and provide refreshment,—for they would have been hoarse and faint if they had gone on much longer. Such a happy procession as filed away into the little dining-room ! Mr. March proudly escorted " Mrs. Laurence " ; Mrs. March as proudly leaned on the arm of

I

" my son " ; the old gentleman took Jo with a whispered
" You must be my girl now," and a glance at the empty
corner by the fire, that made Jo whisper back, with
trembling lips, " I'll try to fill her place, sir."

Amy, who was handed about like refreshments, returned
to the parlour on Father Laurence's arm ; the others
paired off as before, and this arrangement left Jo companion-
less. She did not mind it at the minute, for she lingered
to answer Hannah's eager inquiry—

" Will Miss Amy ride in her coop (*coupé*), and use all them
lovely silver dishes that's stored away over yander ? "

" Shouldn't wonder if she drove six white horses and
wore diamonds and point-lace every day. Teddy thinks
nothing too good for her," returned Jo, with satisfaction.

" No more there is ? Will you have hash or fish-balls
for breakfast ? " asked Hannah.

" I don't care," and Jo shut the door, feeling that food
was an uncongenial topic just then. A sudden sense of
loneliness came over her, so strongly that she looked about
her with dim eyes, as if to find something to lean upon—
for even Teddy had deserted her. Then she drew her hand
over her eyes and had just managed to call up a smile,
when there came a knock at the porch door.

She opened it with hospitable haste, and started as if
another ghost had come to surprise her,—for there stood a
stout gentleman, beaming on her from the darkness like a
midnight sun.

" Oh, Mr. Bhaer, I *am* so glad to see you ! " cried Jo,
with a clutch, as if she feared the night would swallow him
up before she could get him in.

" And I to see Miss Marsch,—but no, you haf a party— "
and the Professor paused as the sound of voices and the
tap of dancing feet came down to them.

" No, we haven't,—only the family. My brother and
sister have just come home, and we are all very happy.
Come in, and make one of us."

Though a very social man, I think Mr. Bhaer would have
gone decorously away, and come again another day ; but
how could he when Jo shut the door behind him, and bereft
him of his hat ? Perhaps her face had something to do
with it, for she forgot to hide her joy at seeing him, and
showed it with a frankness that proved irresistible to the
solitary man, whose welcome far exceeded his boldest hopes.

" If I shall not be Monsieur De Trop I will so gladly see hem all. You haf been ill, my friend ? "

He put the question abruptly, for, as Jo hung up his coat, the light fell on her face, and he saw a change in it.

" Not ill, but sorrowful ; we have had trouble since I saw you last."

" Ah, yes, I know ! my heart was sore for you when I heard that " ; and he shook hands again with such a sympathetic face, that Jo felt as if no comfort could equal the look of the kind eyes, the grasp of the big, warm hand.

" Father, mother, this is my friend, Professor Bhaer," she said, with a face and tone of such irrepressible pride and pleasure, that she might as well have blown a trumpet and opened the door with a flourish.

If the stranger had had any doubts about his reception, they were set at rest in a minute by the cordial welcome he received. Everyone greeted him kindly, for Jo's sake, at first, but very soon they liked him for his own. Mr. Bhaer sat looking about him with the air of a traveller who knocks at a strange door, and, when it opens, finds himself at home. The children went to him like bees to a honey-pot ; and, establishing themselves on each knee, proceeded to captivate him by rifling his pockets and investigating his watch, with juvenile audacity. The women telegraphed their approval to one another, and Mr. March, feeling that he had got a kindred spirit, opened his choicest stores for his guest's benefit, while silent John listened and enjoyed the talk and Mr. Laurence found it impossible to go to sleep.

Jo quite glowed with triumph when Teddy got quenched in an argument, and thought to herself, as she watched her father's absorbed face, " How he would enjoy having such a man as my Professor to talk with, every day ! " Lastly, Mr. Bhaer was dressed in a new suit of black ; his bushy hair had been cut, and smoothly brushed, but didn't stay in order long, for, in exciting moments, he rumpled it up in the droll way he used to do, and Jo liked it rampantly erect, better than flat, because she thought it gave his fine forehead a Jove-like aspect. Poor Jo ! how she did glorify that plain man, as she sat knitting away so quietly, yet letting nothing escape her—not even the fact that Mr. Bhaer actually had gold sleeve-buttons in his immaculate wristbands.

" Dear old fellow ; he couldn't have got himself up with

more care if he'd been going a-wooing," said Jo to herself ;
and then a sudden thought, born of the words, made her
blush so dreadfully, that she had to drop her ball, and go
down after it, to hide her face.

"We must have our sing in the good old way, for we are
all together again, once more," said Jo, feeling that a good
shout would be a vent for the emotions of her soul.

They were not *all* there ; but no one found the words
thoughtless or untrue ; for Beth still seemed among them
invisible, but dearer than ever.   The little chair stood in its
old place ; the tidy-basket was still on its accustomed shelf ;
the beloved instrument, seldom touched now, had not been
moved ; and above it Beth's face looked down upon them,
seeming to say, "Be happy ! I am here."

"Play something, Amy ; let them hear how you have
improved," said Laurie, with pride in his promising pupil.

But Amy whispered as she twirled the faded stool—

"Not to-night, dear ; I can't show off to-night."

But she did show something better than brilliance or
skill, for she sang Beth's songs, with a tender music in her
voice which the best master could not have taught.   The
room was very still when the clear voice failed suddenly,
at the last line of Beth's favourite hymn.   It was hard
to say—

"Earth hath no sorrow that heaven cannot heal "

And Amy leaned against her husband, feeling that home
was not perfect without Beth's kiss.

"Now we must finish with Mignon's song, for Mr. Bhaer
sings that," said Jo, before the pause grew painful ; and
Mr. Bhaer cleared his throat with a gratified "hem," as
he stepped into the corner where Jo stood, saying—

"You will sing with me ; we go excellently well together."

A pleasing fiction, by the way, for Jo had no more idea
of music than a grasshopper ; but it didn't much matter,
for Mr. Bhaer sang like a true German, heartily and well ;
and Jo soon subsided into a subdued hum, that she might
listen to the mellow voice that seemed to sing for her alone.

"Know'st thou the land where the citron blooms ? "

used to be the Professor's favourite line ; for "das land "

meant Germany to him ; but now he seemed to dwell, with
peculiar warmth and melody, upon the words—

" There, oh there, might I with thee, Oh my beloved, go ; "

and one listener was so thrilled by the tender invitation,
that she longed to say she did know the land, and would
joyfully depart thither whenever he liked.

The song was considered a great success, and the singer
bashfully retired, covered with laurels.   But a few minutes
afterwards, he forgot his manners entirely, and stared at
Amy putting on her bonnet, when Laurie said, in his most
gracious manner, at parting—

" My wife and I are very glad to meet you, sir ; please
remember that there is always a welcome waiting for you,
over the way."

Then the Professor thanked him so heartily that Laurie
thought him the most delightfully demonstrative old fellow
he had ever met.

" I too shall go ; but I shall gladly come again, if you
will gif me leave, dear madame, for a little business will
keep me here some days."

He spoke to Mrs. March, but he looked at Jo ; and the
mother's voice gave as cordial an assent as did the daughter's
eyes ; for Mrs. March was not so blind to her children's
interest as Mrs. Moffat supposed.

" I suspect that is a wise man," remarked Mr. March
from the hearth-rug, after the last guest had gone.

" I know he is a good one," added Mrs. March, with
decided approval, as she wound up the clock.

" I thought you'd like him," was all Jo said, as she
slipped away to bed.

She wondered what the business was that brought Mr.
Bhaer to the city, but had she seen his face when, safe in
his own room, he looked at the picture of a severe young
lady, with a good deal of hair, it might have thrown some
light upon the subject, especially when he turned off the
gas, and kissed the picture in the dark.

CHAPTER XXI

MY LORD AND LADY

" PLEASE, Madam Mother, could you lend me my wife for half an hour ?   The luggage has come, and I've been making hay of Amy's Paris finery, trying to find some things I want," said Laurie, coming in the next day to find Mrs. Laurence sitting in her mother's lap, as if being made " the baby " again.

" Certainly ; go, dear ; I forget that you have any home but this," and Mrs. March pressed the hand that wore the wedding-ring, as if asking pardon for her maternal covetousness.

" What are you going to do with yourselves after you get settled ? " asked Jo, buttoning Amy's cloak as she used to button her pinafores.

" We have our plans ; we don't mean to say much about them yet, because we are such very new brooms, but we don't intend to be idle.   I'm going into business with a devotion that shall delight grandpa, and prove to him that I'm not spoilt."

" And Amy, what is she going to do ? " asked Mrs. March, well pleased at Laurie's decision, and the energy with which he spoke.

" After doing the civil all round, and airing our best bonnet, we shall astonish you by the elegant hospitalities of our mansion and the beneficial influence we shall exert over the world at large.   That's about it, isn't it, Madame Recamier ? " asked Laurie, with a quizzical look at Amy.

" Time will show.   Come away, Impertinence, and don't shock my family by calling me names before their faces," answered Amy, resolving that there should be a home with a good wife in it before she set up a *salon* as a queen of society.

" How happy those children seem together ! " observed Mr. March, finding it difficult to become absorbed in his Aristotle after the young couple had gone.

" Yes, and I think it will last," added Mrs. March, with the expression of a pilot who has brought a ship safely into port.

" I know it will. Happy Amy ! " and Jo sighed, then smiled as Professor Bhaer opened the gate with an impatient push.

Later in the evening, Laurie said suddenly to his wife who was flitting about, arranging her new art treasures.

" Mrs. Laurence."

" My Lord ! "

" That man intends to marry our Jo ! "

" I hope so ; don't you, dear ? "

" Well, my love, I consider him a trump, but I do wish he was a little younger and richer."

" Now, Laurie, don't be worldly-minded. If they love one another it doesn't matter a particle how old they are, nor how poor. Women *never* should marry for money— "

Amy caught herself up short as the words escaped her, and looked at her husband, who replied with malicious gravity—

" Certainly not, though if my memory serves me, you once thought it your duty to make a rich match ; that accounts, perhaps, for your marrying a good-for-nothing like me."

" Oh, my dearest boy, don't, don't say that ! I forgot you were rich when I said ' Yes.' I'd have married you if you hadn't a penny, and I sometimes wish you *were* poor that I might show how much I love you " ; and Amy, who was very dignified in public and very fond in private, gave convincing proofs of the truth of her words.

" You don't really think I'm such a mercenary creature as I tried to be once, do you ? It would break my heart, if you didn't believe that I'd gladly pull in the same boat with you, even if you had to get your living by rowing on the lake."

" Am I an idiot and a brute ? How could I think so when you refused a richer man for me, and won't let me give you half I want to now, when I have the right ? I trembled for you at one time, but I was not disappointed, for the daughter was true to the mother's teaching. I told mamma so yesterday, and she looked as grateful as if I'd given her a cheque for a million, to be spent in charity. You are not listening to my moral remarks, Mrs. Laurence,"—

and Laurence paused, for Amy's eyes had an absent look, though fixed upon his face.

"Yes I am, and admiring your chin at the same time. Don't laugh—but your nose is *such* a comfort to me," and Amy softly caressed the well-cut feature with artistic satisfaction.

Laurie had received many compliments in his life, but never one that suited him better, as he plainly showed, though he did laugh at his wife's peculiar taste, while she said slowly—

"May I ask you a question, dear?"

"Of course you may."

"Shall you care if Jo does marry Mr. Bhaer?"

"Oh, that's the trouble, is it? Not being a dog in the manger, but the happiest fellow alive, I assure you I can dance at Jo's wedding with a heart as light as my heels."

Amy looked up at him, and was satisfied.

"I wish we could do something for that capital old Professor. Couldn't we invent a rich relation, who shall obligingly die out there in Germany, and leave him a little fortune?" said Laurie, when they began to pace up and down the long drawing-room, arm-in-arm, as they were fond of doing, in memory of the château garden.

"Jo would find us out, and spoil it all; she is very proud of him, just as he is, and said yesterday that she thought poverty was a beautiful thing."

"Bless her dear heart, she won't think so when she has a literary husband, and a dozen little professors and professorins to support. While I was dawdling about abroad, I saw a good many talented young fellows making all sorts of sacrifices, and enduring real hardships, that they might realise their dreams. Splendid fellows, some of them, so full of courage, patience, and ambition, that I was ashamed of myself, and longed to give them a right good lift. Those are people whom it's a satisfaction to help."

"Yes, indeed; and there's another class who suffer in silence; I belonged to it, before you made a princess of me. Ambitious girls have a hard time, Laurie, and often have to see youth, health, and precious opportunities go by, just for want of a little help at the right minute. People have been very kind to me, and whenever I see girls struggling along as we used to do, I want to put out my hand and help them, as I was helped."

" And so you shall, like an angel as you are ! " cried Laurie, resolving to found and endow an institution, for the express benefit of young women with artistic tendencies. Will you be a little Dorcas, going about emptying a big basket of comforts, and filling it up with good deeds ? "

" With all my heart, if you will be a brave St. Martin, stopping, as you ride gallantly through the world, to share your cloak with the beggar."

" It's a bargain, and we shall get the best of it ! "

So the young pair shook hands on it and then paced happily on again, feeling that their hearts were more closely knit together by a love which could remember those less blessed than they.

CHAPTER XXII

DAISY AND DEMI

I CANNOT feel that I have done my duty as historian of the March family, without devoting at least one chapter to the two most important members of it,—Daisy and Demi. Of course they were the most remarkable children ever born ; as will be shown when I mention that they walked at eight months, talked fluently at twelve months, and at two years they took their places at table, and behaved with a propriety which charmed all beholders. At three Daisy demanded a " needler," and actually made a bag with four stitches in it ; she likewise set up housekeeping in the sideboard, and managed a microscopic cooking-stove with a skill that brought tears of pride to Hannah's eyes, while Demi learned his letters with his grandfather, who invented a new mode of teaching the alphabet by forming the letters with his arms and legs,—thus uniting gymnastics for head and heels.

Though utterly unlike in character, the twins got on remarkably well together, and seldom quarrelled more than thrice a day. Of course, Demi tyrannized over Daisy, and gallantly defended her from every other aggressor; while Daisy made a galley-slave of herself, and adored her brother as the one perfect being in the world. A rosy chubby, sunshiny little soul was Daisy, who found her way to everybody's heart, and nestled there.

" Me loves evvybody," she once said, opening her arms, with her spoon in one hand, and her mug in the other, as if eager to embrace the whole world.

As she grew, her mother began to feel that the Dovecote would be blest by the presence of an inmate as serene and loving as that which had helped to make the old house home. Demi was of an inquiring turn, wanting to know everything, and often getting much disturbed, because he could not get satisfactory answers to his perpetual " Why ? " He also possessed a philosophic bent, to the great delight of his grandfather.

" What makes my legs go, Dranpa ? " asked the young philosopher, surveying those active portions of his frame with a meditative air, while resting after a go-to-bed frolic one night.

" It's your little mind, Demi," replied the sage, stroking the yellow head respectfully.

" What is a little mine ? "

" It is something which makes your body move, as the spring made the wheels go in my watch when I showed it to you."

" Open me ; I want to see it go wound."

" I can't do that any more than you could open the watch. God winds you up, and you go till he stops you."

Demi felt his back, as if expecting to find it like that of the watch, and then gravely remarked—

" I dess Dod does it when I's asleep."

A careful explanation followed, to which he listened so attentively that his anxious grandmother said—

" My dear, do you think it wise to talk about such things to that baby ? He's beginning to ask the most unanswerable questions."

" If he is old enough to ask the questions he is old enough to receive true answers. These children are wiser than we are, and I have no doubt the boy understands every word I have said to him. No, Demi, tell me where you keep your mind ? "

If the boy had replied like Alcibiades. " By the gods,

Socrates, I cannot tell," his grandfather would not have been surprised, but when, after standing a moment on one leg, like a meditative young stork, he answered, in a tone of calm conviction, "In my little belly," the old gentleman could only join in grandma's laugh, and dismiss the class in metaphysics.

Aunt Dodo was chief playmate and *confidante* of both children, and the trio turned the little house topsy-turvy. Aunt Amy was as yet only a name to them, Aunt Beth soon faded into a pleasantly vague memory, but Aunt Dodo was a living reality, and they made the most of her, for which compliment she was deeply grateful. But when Mr. Bhaer came, Jo neglected her playfellows, and dismay and desolation fell upon their little souls. Daisy, who was fond of going about peddling kisses, lost her best customer and became bankrupt ; Demi, with infantile penetration, soon discovered that Dodo liked to play with " the bear-man," better than she did with him ; but, though hurt, he concealed his anguish, for he hadn't the heart to insult a rival who kept a mine of chocolate drops in his waistcoat pocket, and a watch that could be taken out of its case and freely shaken by ardent admirers.

Mr. Bhaer came in one evening to pause on the threshold of the study, astonished by the spectacle that met his eye. Prone upon the floor lay Mr. March, with his respectable legs in the air, and beside him, likewise prone, was Demi, trying to imitate the attitude with his own short, scarlet-stockinged legs ; both grovellers so seriously absorbed that they were unconscious of spectators, till Mr. Bhaer laughed his sonorous laugh, and Jo cried out, with a scandalized face,—

" Father, father ! here's the Professor ! "

Down went the black legs, and up came the grey head, as the preceptor said, with undisturbed dignity—

" Good evening, Mr. Bhaer. Excuse me for a moment,— we are just finishing our lesson. Now Demi, make the letter, and tell its name."

"I knows him," and, after a few convulsive efforts, the red legs took the shape of a pair of compasses, and the intelligent pupil triumphantly shouted, " It's a We, Drandpa, it's a We ! "

" He's a born Weller," laughed Jo, as her parent gathered himself up, and her nephew tried to stand on his head, as the only mode of expressing his satisfaction that school was over.

"What have you been at to-day, bübchen?" asked Mr. Bhaer, picking up the gymnast.

"Me went to see little Mary."

"And what did you get there?"

"I kissed her," began Demi, with artless frankness.

"Prut! thou beginnest early. What did the little Mary say to that?" asked Mr. Bhaer, continuing to confess the young sinner, who stood upon his knee, exploring the waistcoat pocket.

"Oh, she liked it and she kissed me, and I liked it. *Don't* little boys like little girls?" added Demi, with his mouth full.

"You precocious chick,—who put that into your head?" said Jo, enjoying the innocent revelations as much as the Professor.

"'Tisn't in mine head, it's in mine mouf," answered literal Demi, thinking she alluded to confectionery, not ideas.

"Thou shouldst save some for the little friend; sweets to the sweet, mannling," and Mr. Bhaer offered Jo some, with a look that made her wonder if chocolate was not the nectar drunk by the gods. Demi also saw the smile and artlessly inquired—

"Do great boys like great girls, too, 'Fessor?"

Like young Washington, Mr. Bhaer "couldn't tell a lie"; so he gave the somewhat grave reply, that he believed they did, sometimes, in a tone that made Mr. March put down his clothes-brush, glance at Jo's retiring face, and then sink into his chair, looking as if the "precocious chick" had put an idea into *his* head that was both sweet and sour.

Why Dodo, when she caught him in the china-closet half an hour afterwards, nearly squeezed the breath out of his little body with a tender embrace, instead of shaking him for being there, and why she followed up this novel performance by the unexpected gift of a big slice of bread and jelly, remained one of the problems which Demi was forced to leave unsolved for ever.

CHAPTER XXIII

UNDER THE UMBRELLA

WHILE Laurie and Amy were taking conjugal strolls over velvet carpets, as they planned a blissful future, Mr. Bhaer and Jo were enjoying promenades of a different sort, along muddy roads and sodden fields.

" I always do take a walk towards evening, and I don't know why I should give it up, just because I often happen to meet the Professor on his way out," said Jo to herself, after two or three encounters ; for, though there were two paths to Meg's, whichever one she took she was sure to meet him, either going or returning. He was always walking rapidly, and never seemed to see her till quite close, when he would look as if his short-sighted eyes had failed to recognise the approaching lady till that moment. Then, if she was going to Meg's, he always had something for the babies ; if her face was turned homeward, he had merely strolled down to see the river, and was just returning, unless they were tired of his frequent calls. Under the circumstances, what could Jo do, but greet him civilly, and invite him in ?

By the second week, everyone knew perfectly well what was going on, yet everyone tried to look as if they were stone-blind to the changes in Jo's face—never asked why she sang about her work, did up her hair three times a day, and got so blooming with her evening exercise ; and no one seemed to have the slightest suspicion that Professor Bhaer, while talking philosophy with the father, was giving the daughter lessons in love.

For a fortnight, the Professor came and went with lover-like regularity ; then he stayed away for three whole days, and made no sign—a proceeding which caused Jo to become pensive, at first, and then,—alas for romance,—very cross.

" Disgusted, I dare say, and gone home as suddenly as he came. It's nothing to me, of course ; but I *should* think he would have come and bid us good-bye, like a gentleman,' she said to herself, as she put on her things for the customary walk one dull afternoon.

" You'd better take the little umbrella, dear ; it looks like rain," said her mother, observing that she had on her new bonnet.

" Yes, Marmee ; do you want anything in town ? I've got to get some paper," returned Jo, pulling out the bow under her chin, before the glass, as an excuse for not looking at her mother.

" Yes ; I want some twilled silesia, a paper of number nine needles, and two yards of narrow lavender ribbon. Have you got your thick boots on ? "

" I believe so," answered Jo, absently.

" If you happen to meet Mr. Bhaer, bring him home to tea ; I quite long to see the dear man," added Mrs. March. Jo *heard* that, but made no answer, except to kiss her mother, and walk rapidly away, thinking with a glow of gratitude, in spite of her heart-ache—

" How good she is to me ! What *do* girls do who haven't any mothers to help them through their troubles ! "

A drop of rain on her cheek recalled her thoughts from baffled hopes to ruined ribbons ; for the drops continued to fall, and being a woman as well as a lover, she felt that, though it was too late to save her heart, she might her bonnet. Now she remembered the little umbrella, which she had forgotten to take in her hurry to be off ; but regret was unavailing, and nothing could be done but borrow one, or submit to a drenching.

" It serves me right ! What business had I to put on all my best things, and come philandering down here, hoping to see the Professor ? Jo, I'm ashamed of you ! You shall do your errands in the rain ; and if you catch your death, and ruin your bonnet, it's no more than you deserve. Now then ! "

With that she had rushed across the street so impetuously, that she narrowly escaped annihilation from a passing truck, and precipitated herself into the arms of a stately old gentleman, who said, " I beg pardon, ma'am," and looked mortally offended. Somewhat daunted, Jo righted herself, and hurried on, with increasing dampness about the ankles, and much clashing of umbrellas overhead. The fact that a somewhat dilapidated blue one remained stationary above the unprotected bonnet, attracted her attention ; and, looking up, she saw Mr. Bhaer looking down.

" I feel to know the strong-minded lady who goes so bravely under many horse-noses, and so fast through much mud. What do you down here, my friend ? "

" I'm shopping."

Mr. Bhaer smiled, as he glanced from the pickle-factory on one side, to the wholesale hide and leather concern on the other ; but he only said, politely,—

" You haf no umbrella ; may I go also, and take for you the bundles ? "

" Yes, thank you."

Jo's cheeks were as red as her ribbon, and she wondered what he thought of her ; but she didn't care, for in a minute she found herself walking away, arm-in-arm with her Professor, feeling as if the sun had suddenly burst out with uncommon brilliance, and that one thoroughly happy woman was paddling through the wet that day.

" We thought you had gone," said Jo, hastily.

" Did you believe that I should go with no farewell to those who haf been so kind to me ? " he asked, so reproach-fully, that she felt as if she had insulted him by the suggestion, and answered, heartily,—

" No, I didn't ; I knew you were busy about your own affairs, but we rather missed you,—father and mother especially."

" And you ? "

" I'm always glad to see you, sir."

In her anxiety to keep her voice quite calm, Jo made it rather cool, and the frosty little monosyllable at the end seemed to chill the Professor, for his smile vanished, as he said, gravely,—

" I thank you, and come one time more before I go."

" You *are* going, then ? "

" I haf no longer any business here ; it is done."

" Successfully, I hope ? " said Jo, for the bitterness of disappointment was in that short reply of his.

" I ought to think so, for I haf a way opened to me by which I can make my bread and gif my Jünglings much help."

" Tell me, please ! I like to know all about the—the boys," said Jo eagerly.

"That is so kind, I gladly tell you. My friends find for me a place in a college, where I teach as at home, and earn enough to make the way smooth for Franz and Emil. For this I should be grateful, should I not?"

"Indeed you should! How splendid it will be to have you doing what you like, and be able to see you often, and the boys—" cried Jo, clinging to the lads as an excuse for the satisfaction she could not help betraying.

"Ah, but we shall not meet often, I fear; this place is at the West."

"So far away!" and Jo left her skirts to their fate, as if it didn't matter now what became of her clothes or herself.

Mr. Bhaer could read several languages, but he had not learned to read women yet. He flattered himself that he knew Jo pretty well, and was, therefore, much amazed by the contradictions of voice, face, and manner, which she showed him in rapid succession that day,—for she was in half-a-dozen different moods in the course of half an hour. On hearing his destination, she had said, "So far away!" in a tone of despair that lifted him on to a pinnacle of hope; but the next minute she tumbled him down again by observing, like one entirely absorbed in the matter,—

"Here's the place for my errands; will you come in? It won't take long."

Jo wished to impress her escort with the neatness and despatch with which she would accomplish the business, but owing to the flutter she was in, everything went amiss. She forgot the silesia was to be "twilled" till it was cut off, and covered herself with confusion by asking for lavender ribbon at the calico counter. Mr. Bhaer stood by, watching her blush and blunder; and, as he watched, his own bewilderment seemed to subside, for he was beginning to see that on some occasions women, like dreams, go by contraries.

When they came out, he put the parcel under his arm with a more cheerful aspect, and splashed through the puddles as if he rather enjoyed it, on the whole.

"Should we not do a little shopping for the babies, and haf a farewell feast to-night if I go for my last call at your so pleasant home?" he asked, stopping before a window full of fruit and flowers.

"What will we buy?" said Jo, ignoring the latter part

of his speech, and sniffing the mingled odours with an affectation of delight, as they went in.

"Hamburg grapes; yes, we shall surely drink to the Fatherland in those?"

Jo frowned upon that piece of extravagance, whereat Mr. Bhaer confiscated her purse, produced his own, and finished the marketing by buying several pounds of grapes, a pot of daisies, and a jar of honey, to be regarded in the light of a demi-john. Then, distorting his pockets with the knobby bundles, and giving her the flowers to hold, he put up the old umbrella, and they travelled on again.

"Miss Marsch, I haf a great favour to ask of you," began the Professor, after a moist promenade of half a block.

"Yes, sir," and Jo's heart began to beat so hard she was afraid he would hear it.

"I am bold to say it in spite of the rain, because so short a time remains to me."

"Yes, sir," and Jo nearly smashed the small flower-pot with the sudden squeeze she gave it.

"I wish to get a little dress for my Tina, and I am too stupid to go alone. Will you kindly gif me a word of taste and help."

"Yes, sir," and Jo felt as cool all of a sudden, as if she had stepped into a refrigerator.

"Perhaps also a shawl for Tina's mother, she is so poor, and the husband is such a care,—yes, yes, a thick, warm shawl would be a friendly thing to take the little mother."

"I'll do it with pleasure, Mr. Bhaer. I'm going very fast, and he's getting dearer every minute," added Jo to herself; then, with a mental shake, she entered into the business with an energy which was pleasant to behold.

Mr. Bhaer left it all to her, so she chose a pretty gown for Tina, and then ordered out the shawls. The clerk, being a married man, condescended to take an interest in the couple, who appeared to be shopping for their family.

"Your lady may prefer this; it's a superior article," he said, shaking out a comfortable grey shawl, and throwing it over Jo's shoulders.

"Does this suit you, Mr. Bhaer?" she asked, turning her back to him, and feeling grateful for the chance of hiding her face.

"Excellently well, we will haf it," answered the Professor, smiling to himself, as he paid for it, while Jo

K

continued to rummage the counters, like a confirmed bargain-hunter.

"Now shall we go home?" he asked, as if the words were very pleasant to him.

"Yes, it's late, and I'm *so* tired." Jo's voice was more pathetic than she knew, for now the sun seemed to have gone in as suddenly as it came out. Mr. Bhaer was going away; he only cared for her as a friend, it was all a mistake, and the sooner it was over the better. With this idea in her head, she hailed an approaching omnibus with such a hasty gesture that the daisies flew out of the pot, and were badly damaged.

"That is not our omniboos,' said the Professor, waving the vehicle away, and stooping to pick up the poor little posies.

"I beg your pardon, I didn't see the name distinctly. Never mind, I'm used to plodding in the mud," returned Jo, blinking hard, because she would have died rather than wipe her eyes.

Mr. Bhaer saw the drops on her cheeks, though she turned her head away; the sight seemed to touch him very much, for stooping down, he asked in a tone that meant a great deal,—

"Heart's dearest, why do you cry?"

Now if Jo had not been new to this sort of thing she would have said she had a cold in her head, or told any other feminine fib proper to the occasion; instead of which that undignified creature answered,—

"Because you are going away."

"Ah, my Gott, that is *so* good!" cried Mr. Bhaer. "Jo, I haf nothing but much love to gif you; I came to see if you would care for it, and I waited to be sure that I was something more than a friend. Am I?"

"Oh yes!" said Jo, and he was quite satisfied, for she folded both hands over his arm, and looked up at him with an expression that plainly showed how happy she would be to walk through life beside him, even though she had no better shelter than the old umbrella, if he carried it.

It was certainly proposing under difficulties, for even if he had desired to do so, Mr. Bhaer could not go down upon his knees, on account of the mud, neither could he offer Jo his hand, except figuratively, for both were full; much less could he indulge in tender demonstrations in the open

street, though he was near it ; so the only way in which
he could express his rapture was to look at her, with an
expression which glorified his face to such a degree that
there actually seemed to be little rainbows in the drops
that sparkled on his chin.

Passers-by probably thought them a pair of harmless
lunatics, for they entirely forgot to hail a bus, and strolled
leisurely along, oblivious of deepening dusk and fog. The
Professor looked as if he had conquered a kingdom, and
the world had nothing more to offer him in the way of
bliss, while Jo trudged beside him, feeling as if her place
had always been there, and wondering how she ever could
have chosen any other lot. Of course, she was the first
to speak—intelligently, I mean, for the emotional remarks
which followed her impetuous " Oh yes ! " were not of a
coherent or reportable character.

" Friedrich, why didn't you—"

" Ah, heaven ! she gifs me the name that no one speaks
since Minna died ! " cried the Professor, pausing in a
puddle to regard her with grateful delight.

" I always call you so to myself ; but I won't unless
you like it."

" Like it ! it is more sweet to me than I can tell. Say
' thou,' also, and I shall say your language is as beautiful
as mine."

" Well, then, why didn't thou tell me all this sooner ? "
asked Jo, bashfully.

" Now I shall haf to show thee all my heart, and I so
gladly will, because thou must take care of it hereafter.
See, then, my Jo—ah, the dear, funny little name !—I had
a wish to tell something the day I said good-bye, in New
York ; but I thought the handsome friend was betrothed
to thee, and so I spoke not. Woulds't thou have said
' Yes ' then, if I *had* spoken ? "

" I'm afraid not, for I didn't have any heart just
then."

" Prut ! that I do not believe. Ah, well, ' Die erste
Liebe ist die beste ; ' but that I should not expect."

" Yes, the first love *is* the best ; so be contented, for I
never had another. Teddy was only a boy, and soon got
over his little fancy," said Jo, anxious to correct the
Professor's mistake.

" Good ! then I shall rest happy, and be sure that thou

givest me all. I haf waited so long, I am grown selfish,
as thou wilt find, Professorin."

" I like that," cried Jo, delighted with her new name.
" Now tell me what brought you just when I most wanted
you ? "

" This,"—and Mr. Bhaer took a paper out of his pocket.

" I found it by chance ; I knew it by the names and the
initials, and in it there was one little verse that seemed to
call me. Read and find him ; I will see that you go not
in the wet."

Jo obeyed, and hastily skimmed through the lines
which she had christened—

" IN THE GARRET.

" Four little chests all in a row,
　　Dim with dust, and worn by time,
All fashioned and filled, long ago,
　　By children now in their prime.
Four little keys hung side by side,
　　With faded ribbons, brave and gay,
When fastened there with childish pride,
　　Long ago, on a rainy day.
Four little names, one on each lid,
　　Carved out by a boyish hand,
And underneath, there lieth hid
　　Histories of the happy band
Once playing here, and pausing oft
　　To hear the sweet refrain,
That came and went on the roof aloft,
　　In the falling summer rain.

" ' Meg ' on the first lid, smooth and fair,
　　I look in with loving eyes,
For folded here, with well-known care,
　　A goodly gathering lies—
The record of a peaceful life,
　　Gifts to gentle child and girl,
A bridal gown, lines to a wife,
　　A tiny shoe, a baby curl.
No toys in this first chest remain
　　For all are carried away,
In their old age, to join again
　　In another small Meg's play.

Ah, happy mother! well I know
   You hear like a sweet refrain,
Lullabies ever soft and low,
   In the falling summer rain.

'' Jo' on the next lid, scratched and worn,
   And within a motley store
Of headless dolls, of school-books torn,
   Birds and beasts that speak no more.
Spoils brought home from the fairy ground
   Only trod by youthful feet,
Dreams of a future never found,
   Memories of a past still sweet ;
Half-writ poems, stories wild,
   April letters, warm and cold,
Diaries of a wilful child,
   Hints of a woman early old ;
A woman in a lonely home,
   Hearing like a sad refrain,—
' Be worthy love, and love will come,'
   In the falling summer rain.

" My ' Beth!' the dust is always swept
   From the lid that bears your name,
As if by loving eyes that wept,
   By careful hands that often came.
Death canonized for us one saint,
   Ever less human than divine,
And still we lay, with tender plaint,
   Relics in this household shrine.
The silver bell, so seldom rung,
   The little cap which last she wore,
The fair, dead Catherine that hung
   By angels borne above her door ;
The songs she sang, without lament,
   In her prison-house of pain,
For ever are they sweetly blent
   With the falling summer rain.

" Upon the last lid's polished field—
   Legend now both fair and true—
A gallant knight bears on his shield,
   ' Amy,' in letters gold and blue.

Within the snoods that bound her hair,
  Slippers that have danced their last,
Faded flowers laid by with care,
  Fans whose airy toils are past—
Gay valentines all ardent flames,
  Trifles that have borne their part
In girlish hopes, and fears, and shames
  The record of a maiden heart,
Now learning fairer, truer spells,
  Hearing, like a blithe refrain
The silver sound of bridal bells
  In the falling summer rain.

Four little chests all in a row,
  Dim with dust, and worn by time,
Four women, taught by weal and woe,
  To love and labour in their prime.
Four sisters, parted for an hour,—
  None lost, one only gone before,
Made by love's immortal power,
  Nearest and dearest evermore.
Oh, when these hidden stores of ours
  Lie open to the Father's sight,
May they be rich in golden hours,—
  Deeds that show fairer for the light.
Lives whose brave music long shall ring
  Like a spirit-stirring strain,
Souls that shall gladly soar and sing
  In the long sunshine, after rain.

                                    " J. M."

  " It's very bad poetry, but I wrote it one day when
I was very lonely, and had a good cry on a rag-bag. I
never thought it would go where it could tell tales," said
Jo, tearing up the verses the Professor had treasured so
long.

  " Let it go,—it has done its duty,—and I will haf a fresh
one when I read the book in which she keeps her secrets,"
said Mr. Bhaer with a smile, as he watched the fragments
fly away on the wind. " Yes," he added earnestly, " I read
that, and I think to myself, ' She has a sorrow, she is
lonely, she would find comfort in true love,' I haf a heart
full, full for her ; shall I not go and say, ' If this is not too

poor a thing to gif for what I shall hope to receive, take it, in Gott's name.' "

" And so you came to find that it was the one precious thing I needed," whispered Jo.

" I had no courage to think that at first, kind as was your welcome to me. But soon I began to hope, and then I said, ' I will haf her, if I die for it,' and so I will ! " cried Mr. Bhaer, with a defiant nod, as if the walls of mist closing round them were barriers which he was to knock down.

" Haf you patience to wait a long time, Jo ? I must help my boys first, because even for you I may not break my word to Minna. Can you forgif that, and be happy, while we hope and wait ? "

" Yes, I know I can ; for we love one another, and that makes all the rest easy to bear. I have my duty also, and my work. I couldn't enjoy myself if I neglected them even for you, so there's no need of hurry or impatience. You can do your part out West, I can do mine here, and both be happy, hoping for the best, and leaving the future to be as God wills."

" Ah ! thou gifest me such hope and courage, and I haf nothing to gif back but a full heart and these empty hands," cried the Professor, quite overcome.

Jo never, never would learn to be proper ; for when he said that as they stood upon the steps, she just put both hands into his, whispering tenderly, " Not empty now ; " and kissed her Friedrich under the umbrella.

CHAPTER XXIV

HARVEST TIME

FOR a year Jo and her Professor worked and waited, hoped and loved ; met occasionally, and wrote such voluminous letters, that the rise in the price of paper was accounted for, Laurie said. The second year began rather soberly,

for their prospect did not brighten, and Aunt March died
suddenly. But when their first sorrow was over,—for they
loved the old lady in spite of her sharp tongue,—they
found they had cause for rejoicing, for she had left
Plumfield to Jo, which made all sorts of joyful things
possible.

" It's a fine old place, and will bring a handsome sum,
for of course you intend to sell it ? " said Laurie, as they
were all talking the matter over, some weeks later.

" No, I don't," was Jo's answer, as she petted the
poodle, whom she had adopted out of respect to his mistress.

" You don't mean to live there ? "

" Yes, I do."

" But, my dear girl, it's an immense house, and will take
a power of money to keep it in order. The garden and
orchard alone need two or three men, and farming isn't in
Bhaer's line, I take it."

" He'll try his hand at it there, if I propose it."

" And you expect to live on the produce of the place ? "

" The crop we are going to raise is a profitable one ; "
and Jo laughed.

" Of what is this fine crop to consist, ma'am ? "

" Boys ! I want to open a school for little lads—with
me to take care of them, and Fritz to teach them."

" Isn't that just like her ? " cried Laurie, appealing to
the family.

" I like it," said Mrs. March, decidedly.

" So do I," added her husband, who welcomed the
thought of trying the Socratic method of education on
youth.

" It's a splendid idea—tell us all about it," cried Mr.
Laurence, who had been longing to lend the lovers a hand,
but knew they would refuse his help.

" I knew you'd stand by me, sir. It's just the place
for boys—the house is big, and the furniture strong and
plain. There's plenty of room for dozens inside, and
splendid grounds outside. They could help in the garden
and orchard—such work is healthy, isn't it, sir ? Then
Fritz can train and teach in his own way, and father will
help him. I can feed, and nurse, and pet, and scold them ;
and mother will be my stand-by. I've always longed for
lots of boys, and never had enough ; now I can fill the
house full, and revel in the little dears to my heart's con-

tent. Think what luxury; Plumfield my own, and a wilderness of boys to enjoy it with me!"

As Jo waved her hands and gave a sigh of rapture, the family went off into a gale of merriment, and Mr. Laurence laughed till they thought he'd have an apoplectic fit.

"I don't see anything funny," she said gravely, when she could be heard. "Nothing could be more natural or proper than for my Professor to open a school, and for me to prefer to reside on my own estate."

"She is putting on airs already," said Laurie, who regarded the idea in the light of a capital joke. "But may I inquire how you intend to support the establishment? If all the pupils are little ragamuffins, I'm afraid your crop won't be profitable, in a worldly sense, Mrs. Bhaer."

"Now, don't be a wet-blanket, Teddy. Of course, I shall have rich pupils also—perhaps, begin with such altogether; then, when I've got a start, I can take a ragamuffin or two, just for a relish. Rich people's children often need care and comfort, as well as poor. I've had experience, too, for haven't I brought up one boy to be a pride and honour to his family?"

"I'll testify that you tried to do it," said Laurie, with a grateful look.

"And I've succeeded beyond my hopes; for here you are, a steady, sensible, business man, doing lots of good with your money, and laying up the blessings of the poor, instead of dollars. Yes, and when I have my flock, I'll just point to you, and say, 'There's your model, my lads.'"

Poor Laurie didn't know where to look as this praise made all faces turn approvingly upon him.

"I say, Jo, that's rather too much," he began, just in his old boyish way. "You have all done more for me than I can ever thank you for, except by doing my best not to disappoint you."

"I do think that families are the most beautiful things in all the world!" burst out Jo, who was in an unusually uplifted frame of mind, just then. "When I have one of my own, I hope it will be as happy as the three I know and love the best."

It was a very astonishing year, altogether, for things seemed to happen in an unusually rapid and delightful manner. Almost before she knew where she was, Jo found herself married and settled at Plumfield. Then a family of six or seven boys sprang up like mushrooms, and flourished surprisingly. Poor boys, as well as rich—for Mr. Laurence was continually finding some touching case of destitution, and begging the Bhaers to take pity on the child, and he would gladly pay a trifle for its support. In this way the sly old gentleman got round Jo, and furnished her with the style of boy in which she delighted.

Of course it was up-hill work at first, and Jo made queer mistakes; but the wise Professor steered her safely into calmer waters, and the most rampant ragamuffin was conquered in the end. How Jo did enjoy her " wilderness of boys," and how poor, dear Aunt March would have lamented had she been there to see the sacred precincts of prim, well-ordered Plumfield over-run with Toms, Dicks and Harrys! It became a boy's paradise, and Laurie suggested that it should be called the " Bhaer-garten," as a compliment to its master, and appropriate to its inhabitants.

It never was a fashionable school, and the Professor did not lay up a fortune, but it *was* just what Jo intended it to be, " a happy, home-like place for boys who needed teaching, care, and kindness." Every room in the big house was soon full, every little plot in the garden soon had its owner, a regular menagerie appeared in barn and shed—for pet animals were allowed—and, three times a day, Jo smiled at her Fritz from the head of a long table lined on either side with rows of happy young faces, which all turned to her with affectionate eyes and hearts full of love for Mother Bhaer."

As the years went by, two little lads of her own came to increase her happiness. Rob, named for grandpa, and Teddy—a happy-go-lucky baby, who seemed to have inherited his papa's sunshiny temper as well as his mother's lively spirit. How they ever grew up alive in that whirlpool of boys, was a mystery to their grandma and aunts; but they flourished like dandelions in spring, and their rough nurses loved and served them well.

There were a great many holidays at Plumfield, and one of the most delightful was the yearly apple-picking—for then the Marches, Laurences, Brookeses, and Bhaers turned out in full force, and made a day of it. Five years after Jo's wedding one of these fruitful festivals occurred.

Everybody was there—everybody laughed and sang, climbed up and tumbled down ; everybody declared that there never had been such a perfect day or such a jolly set to enjoy it—and everyone gave themselves up to the simple pleasures of the hour as freely as if there were no such things as care or sorrow in the world.

Jo was in her element that day, and rushed about with her gown pinned up, her hat anywhere but on her head, and her baby tucked under her arm, ready for any lively adventure which might turn up. Little Teddy bore a charmed life, for nothing ever happened to him, and Jo never felt any anxiety when he was whisked up into a tree by one lad, galloped off on the back of another, or supplied with sour russets by his indulgent papa, who laboured under the delusion that babies could digest anything. She knew that little Ted would turn up again in time, safe and rosy, dirty and serene, and she always received him back with a hearty welcome for Jo loved her babies tenderly.

At four o'clock, Jo and Meg, with a detachment of the bigger boys, set forth the supper on the grass—for an out-of-door tea was always the crowning joy of the day. When no one could eat any more, the Professor proposed the first toast, which was always drunk at such times— " Aunt March, God bless her ! " A toast heartily given by the good man, who never forgot how much he owed her.

" Now, grandma's sixtieth birthday ! Long life to her, with three times three ! "

That was given with a will, as you may well believe ; and the cheering once begun, it was hard to stop it. Demi, as the oldest grandchild, then presented the queen of the day with various gifts, so numerous that they were transported to the festive scene in a wheelbarrow. Funny presents, some of them—for the children's gifts were all their own. Every stitch Daisy's little fingers had put into the handkerchiefs she hemmed, was better than embroidery to Mrs. March ; Demi's shoe-box was a miracle of mechanical skill, though the cover wouldn't shut ; Rob's footstool had a wiggle in its uneven legs, that she declared was very soothing ; and no page of the book Amy's child gave her, was so fair as that on which appeared, in tipsy capitals, the words—" To dear Grandma, from her little Beth."

During this ceremony the boys had mysteriously disappeared; and, when Mrs. March had tried to thank her children, and broken down, while Teddy wiped her eyes on his pinafore, the Professor suddenly began to sing. Then, from above him, voice after voice took up the words, and from tree to tree echoed the music of the unseen choir, as the boys sang, with all their hearts, the little song Jo had written, Laurie set to music, and the Professor trained his lads to give with the best effect. This was something altogether new, and it proved a grand success, for Mrs. March couldn't get over her surprise, and insisted on shaking hands with every one of the featherless birds, after which the boys dispersed for a final lark, leaving Mrs. March and her daughters under the festival tree.

" I don't think I ever ought to call myself ' Unlucky Jo ' again, when my greatest wish has been so beautifully gratified," said Mrs. Bhaer, taking Teddy's little fist out of the milk pitcher, in which he was rapturously churning.

" And yet your life is very different from the one you pictured so long ago. Do you remember our castles in the air ? " asked Amy, smiling as she watched Laurie and John playing cricket with the boys.

" Yes, I remember," answered Jo, " but the life I wanted then seems selfish, lonely and cold to me now. I haven't given up the hope that I may write a good book yet, but I can wait, and I m sure it will be all the better for such experiences and illustrations as these ; " and Jo pointed from the lively lads in the distance to her father, leaning on the Professor's arm, as they walked to and fro in the sunshine, deep in one of the conversations which both enjoyed so much.

" My castle was the most nearly realized of all. I asked for splendid things, to be sure, but in my heart I knew I should be satisfied, if I had a little home, and John, and some dear children like these," and Meg laid her hand on her tall boy's head, with a face full of content.

" My castle is very different from what I planned, but I would not alter it, though, like Jo, I don't relinquish all my artistic hopes. I've begun to model a figure of baby, and Laurie says it is the best thing I've ever done. I mean to do it in marble, so that whatever happens, I may at least keep the image of my little angel."

As Amy spoke, a great tear dropped on the golden hair

of the sleeping child in her arms ; for her one well-beloved daughter was a frail little creature, and the dread of losing her was the shadow over Amy's sunshine.

" She is growing better, I am sure of it, my dear ; don't despond, but hope, and keep happy," said Mrs. March, as tender-hearted Daisy stooped from her knee, to lay her rosy cheek against her little cousin's pale one.

" I never ought to, while I have you to cheer me up, Marmee, and Laurie to take more than half of every burden," replied Amy, warmly. " So, in spite of my one cross, I can say with Meg, ' Thank God, I'm a happy woman.' "

" There's no need for me to say it, for everyone can see that I'm far happier than I deserve," added Jo, glancing from her good husband to her chubby children, tumbling on the grass beside her.

" Yes, Jo, I think your harvest will be a good one," began Mrs. March.

" Not half so good as yours, mother. We never can thank you enough for the patient sowing and reaping you have done," cried Jo, with the loving impetuosity which she never could outgrow.

" I hope there will be more wheat and fewer tares every year," said Amy softly.

" A large sheaf, but I know there's room in your heart or it, Marmee, dear," added Meg's tender voice.

Mrs. March could only stretch out her arms, as if to gather children and grandchildren to herself, and say, with voice full of motherly love :

" My girls, however long you may live, I never can wish you a greater happiness than this ! "

THE END